DEATH ON ROUTE THIRTY SEVEN

by Reginald Gray

Chapter one

It was two thirty on a bright Tuesday afternoon in May. The yellow number thirty-seven double deck bus was travelling along a quiet, tree lined residential road in the more affluent part of town. The well maintained semi-detached houses stood some distance back from the road, mostly behind high hedges and large, recently mown front lawns. The bus wasn't full but there were several people on both decks most of them making their way to the local shopping centre. The bus approached a stop where two women and four men had stepped from the bus shelter towards the kerb in readiness to board.

As the bus drew to a halt the entry and exit doors slid open. The two women climbed the steps at the entry door, touched their travel cards to the reader and made their way to empty seats on the lower deck. Two of the men, however, moved quickly along the pavement to the exit doors in the middle of the bus, jumped aboard and rapidly climbed the stairs to the upper deck. The driver was about to shout to them to come back and pay their fare when the other two men came aboard at the front. As they mounted the step towards the driver they pulled scarves up to their eyes to mask their faces and took guns from their pockets. One of them stood by the driver menacing all on the lower deck with his gun, while the other started to threaten each passenger in turn demanding anything of value.

The whole scene was so unexpected and happened so quickly that not a sound was uttered by the passengers but alarm was clearly written across their faces. Those on the upper deck were facing a similar situation.

A young man sitting close to the exit on the lower deck was the first to move. He stood from his seat and started towards the doors, which were still open, hoping to leave the bus and perhaps get help. Immediately a shot rang out from the gunman standing by the driver and a bullet thudded into the upholstery uncomfortably close to the young man.

Any doubt that the robbers would actually use their guns dissolved at that moment and the young man promptly sat down again. The shot had brought screams from most of the women, and looks of horror and disbelief from all the passengers on the lower deck. Handbags and wallets were quickly opened to reveal their contents to the second gunman who grabbed anything worthwhile and stuffed it into his pockets. The bus driver tried to take advantage of the distraction and made a move for the buttons to close the doors and so make it difficult for the bandits to leave the bus. A second shot from the gunman beside him hit him in the hand before he could reach the buttons causing him excruciating pain.

The gunman demanded that the driver hand over his takings plus everything in his pockets. The second man continued to relieve the passengers of everything they had.

After a few moments the two robbers from the upper deck ran down the stairs and out of the exit door. They rapidly made their way to a car parked a short distance in front of the bus. One of them opened the nearside passenger and rear doors then jumped in to the rear seat slamming the door behind him and opening slightly the offside door. The other man opened the driver's door, leaned in and turned a key already in the ignition and started the engine. He then joined the man in the rear seat leaving the driver's door open. The robber on the lower deck of the bus, who had been taking the passengers valuables, threw the last of the handbags on to the floor of the bus, ran to the car, climbed into the driving seat and started to rev the engine, ready to go.

The gunman who had already shot twice turned to the injured bus driver, pointed the gun at the startled man's head and pulled the trigger for the third time. The driver slumped forward on to the steering wheel where he stayed motionless. The gunman turned, ran down the steps and to the front passenger seat of the waiting car. As the passenger door slammed shut the driver put the engine into gear and the car quickly disappeared from sight down the side streets.

The bus passengers from the upper deck slowly made their way down the stairs, frightened of what they might see. They had heard the shots, of course, but had no idea of what had been happening. Those on the lower deck, stunned into silence, moved quickly to try to help the bus driver but saw surprisingly little blood oozing from a hole in his left temple. The poor man was obviously dead. The young man who had suffered the first warning shot took out a mobile 'phone he had managed to hide from the gunmen and dialled 999.

As the car sped towards town the man in the front passenger seat looked sideways at the driver.

"Slow down." he said, "Don't panic. We don't want to be stopped for speeding, keep within the thirty mile per hour limit."

"Why did you have to shoot him?" the driver almost screamed at him, "When you gave us these guns you said there would be no need to use them, why did you have to shoot him?"

"Just take my word for it that it was necessary," replied the man, "you just concentrate for the time being on your driving and stop getting hysterical. These things happen, sometimes it can't be helped."

"You told us this was going to be a lark, it's turning into a nightmare." shouted the driver, "If you've killed that bus driver we'll all be wanted for murder. Damn, now those lights are changing to red. What do I do?"

"Behave normally and stop. Don't bring attention to us. The police won't be looking for us yet, there hasn't been time for them to get organised."

The driver stopped the car, his fingers drumming nervously on the steering wheel as he stared up at the traffic lights willing them to change to green. As soon as the car had pulled up the two rear doors opened, one slightly later than the other, and the men in the back of the car jumped out and ran off in different directions.

"Bloody idiots," said the man in the front passenger seat, looking round but unable to do anything to stop them, "that's what comes of using amateurs like you three."

"What do we do now?" shouted the driver.

"I'll catch up with them later, don't you worry." said the man, "We've got to get rid of this car, some of the people on that bus may be able to describe it. Carry on with our original plan and make your way round the side streets to the derelict railway sidings."

"Are you sure nobody goes there now?" asked the driver, "I used to spend hours over there when I was a kid. If someone sees us dumping this car there they will soon put two and two together."

"I've studied that place thoroughly; believe me it's deserted these days. You might get a couple of kids rummaging around now and again but they're at school at the moment, or should be. The place I've got in mind can't be seen from the road and the houses are too far away for anyone to see what we're doing anyway. The embankment on the other side hides it from the railway, believe me there's nothing to worry about."

"Nothing to worry about!" shouted the driver, "Robbing bus passengers is one thing, but murder! I don't understand you; I wish I'd never got involved."

"Stop whimpering. Here we are, now make your way to that old building by that pile of junk over there. Try to tuck the car in as close as you can."

The driver manoeuvred the car into the space indicated by his passenger, stopped the engine and reached for the door handle.

"Don't bother with that." the man said.

The driver looked quickly around to see the gun pointed at him.

"You are crazy" he cried, "What do you think you're doing?"

"I'm sorry, Frankie," said the man, "You know too much and I can't trust you to keep quiet. I've shot one man this afternoon another won't make a lot of difference. It'll be easier now those other two idiots have gone. Like I said, I can catch up with them later, you won't be alone."

He pointed the gun at the driver's head and, as Frankie screamed for him to stop, pulled the trigger for the fourth time. Frankie fell forward on to the steering wheel, blood dripping down the dashboard and on to his knees.

The man took a bag from the pocket of his duffle coat and went through the driver's pockets for the loot from the bus which he placed in the bag. He then went into the building and reappeared with two cans of petrol which he proceeded to empty over the body of the driver and the interior and exterior of the car. He took off his own duffle coat and scarf, underneath which he was wearing a sports jacket, and threw them on to the rear seats. He then drew a box of matches and a piece of paper from his trouser pockets, lit the paper and tossed it into the car which immediately erupted in a ball of flame. Without looking back he made his way quickly to the roadway, making sure there was no chance he could be seen, and walked briskly towards the town.

"This is highway robbery in the old style." said Detective Inspector Ted Harty of West Town C.I.D. as he stood by the bus. He looked at the passengers gathered in a sorry group along the pavement.

Detective Inspector Harty was a big man, fifty-one years of age, with a ruddy complexion and sporting a heavy moustache. Dressed in a tweed jacket and green corduroys he had the appearance more of a gentleman farmer than of a detective inspector. 'Harty by name, hearty by nature' was a favourite saying of his. He had been with West Town police force most of his working life and had risen through the ranks. He often reminisced about his early days when he was a bobby on the beat and revelled in telling 'how better things were then'. He loved his job and was respected by all his colleagues for his diligence and the inevitability of a good result in every case he tackled. He would not have fitted in with the ways of a police force in a large city, indeed would not have wanted to, but was well suited to a rural area such as West Town. He was blessed with a loving wife who fully understood the needs of his job and had, more than once in the past, been a tower of strength to him when things hadn't gone too well.

Beside him stood Detective Sergeant Bob Tully, at thirty-one a very different individual to his inspector. He kept himself very fit and would not dream of starting the day without his exercises and the morning jog. He was a handsome man of six feet two inches but had never married. He always dressed soberly and smartly in a dark suit with a tie when on duty. He was ambitious but realised that he could learn a lot from Inspector Harty and was pleased that he had been assigned to this case.

The two men had worked together before and both appreciated the ways and idiosyncrasies of the other.

"First time I've heard of a bus being hijacked." replied the Sergeant, "Shouldn't have thought it would be worth the risk."

"You'd be surprised what people carry in their handbags and wallets." said the Inspector, "Already we know that one chap had over six thousand pounds he was taking to the bank, weekend takings from his shop. Can't say I've known of anything quite like this before though."

The Sergeant turned to watch as the body of the bus driver was taken to a waiting ambulance.

"Why kill the driver?" he asked. "A completely senseless and unnecessary thing to do it seems to me."

"Oh, there could be a number of reasons." replied D.I. Harty. "From all accounts the gunman seemed to be rather trigger happy, it could be a motiveless killing. On the other hand it is possible that the driver could have recognised at least one of the gang and was put out of the way so that he couldn't point the finger. It's also possible, but I should think most unlikely, that the driver was in it too and was shot so that the spoils could be divided between fewer of them."

"If that was the case" said the Sergeant, "we can probably expect more bodies. The whole thing, like most robberies, seems to be motivated by greed and if the greediest has already killed once he won't hesitate to do it again."

"Yes Bob, but as I said, it's unlikely. We can't rule anything out at this stage though. For my own part I'm inclined to think that it was carried out by someone who has worked, and perhaps still works, on the buses and knows the route. They chose an ideal spot, a very quiet road but close enough to town for there to be a reasonable number of passengers."

"How could they know that it would be worthwhile raiding this bus though? They couldn't know who would be on it and what they would be carrying it seems to me a very chancy sort of crime."

"You think about it Bob! People are creatures of habit. They tend to do things automatically week by week almost without thinking about it. Collect their allowances and pensions, take money to the bank, do their weekly shopping. Then they meet each other on the same bus at the same time and talk about what they have done and what they are going to do. On top of that, as I have just said, the shopping centre is only about half a mile from here so the bus is about as full as it's going to be on the quietest part of the route. This crime has been carefully worked out believe me, and it's not going to be an easy one to crack."

"From what you have said Guv, it could also have been carried out by someone who has been a regular passenger and not necessarily a bus driver. In fact a passenger would have a better opportunity to overhear conversations."

"A good point." replied the Inspector "Perhaps we can get some indication from the passengers although, for the most part, people are very unobservant so I don't hold out much hope there. By the way, I don't suppose anybody noticed the car number?"

"No, I'm afraid not! Apparently everything happened very quickly. The double shock of the raid itself and the shooting of the driver meant that nobody thought to look at the car or even had any interest in it."

"Never mind, it was probably stolen anyway. Take the names and addresses of the passengers and ask them to call at the station tomorrow to give statements and details of what was taken. No good doing it now they probably wouldn't know what they were saying. Send them home to get over the shock. Meanwhile you can organise door to door enquiries round here to see if anything was noticed, probably a waste of time but it must be done."

"There's not much more I can do here" he continued, "I'll make my way to the bus depot and see if I can glean anything there."

Chapter two

The television was on in the kitchen as Freda Hollingsworth was preparing her husband's tea. She wasn't really watching it but used it as a sort of background companion. The six o'clock news was being shown when she heard mentioned the name of the bus company her husband worked for. Looking up she saw pictures of the number thirty seven bus cordoned off and police cars around it.

"Stan!" she called out "Are you watching the news? Looks as though something's happened on your route. I missed the beginning but it looks pretty serious. Oh my God! Pete's been killed!"

"What's that?" said Stan coming into the kitchen.

"There's been a robbery or something on one of your buses and Pete's been killed." she repeated, reaching over to turn up the volume on the set.

"Pete? Dead? What do you mean? That can't be right; you must have got it wrong."

"No I wasn't really listening so I missed most of it but they definitely said that the bus driver, Peter Thompson, had been killed, shot I think. His bus had been held up by gangsters and robbed. Doesn't look as though anybody else has been hurt but it seems there was quite a bit of shooting."

"I can't believe it!" exclaimed Stan, "How could that have happened? I'll have to ring the depot and find out what's up. See if they say any more about it on television while I'm on the 'phone, love." He went out to the telephone in the hall to make his call.

After a few moments he returned to the kitchen and said, "It's no good, I can't get through to the depot, I'll have to go down there and see what's going on. I've never known anything like this happen before. OK, we've had trouble from rowdies, and the loonies try to beat us up sometimes but this! A bus hold-up! What's it all coming to? Anything more about it on the TV?"

"No," Freda replied, "they just repeated again at the end of the news that Pete had been killed. Oh, Stan!" she cried "If you hadn't taken the day off it could have been you instead of Pete."

"Don't make me feel worse than I already do." he said, "Pete shouldn't have been on today. He was doing my shift for me. Now, I must go to the depot and see what's happening. I don't know what but there might be something I can do."

"But what about your tea? It's nearly ready."

"Oh, shove it in the oven, I'll have it later, I'm sorry love, but with all this going on I couldn't eat anything now anyway."

With that Stan put on his coat, grabbed the car keys from the hall stand, slammed the front door shut behind him, walked quickly down the front garden path to his car and drove off to the depot.

Harry Davies opened the front door of his house and called out, "Hello Sylv, I'm home. Hope you've got something decent to eat we've had a hell of day down at the depot. Expect you've heard all about it, haven't you?"

Harry Davies was a mechanic at the bus depot and knew both Stan Hollingsworth and the dead driver, Pete Thompson, quite well to talk to although rarely had anything to do with either of them socially outside working hours. He was thirty-eight years old and came, originally, from somewhere in the North of England. He was short and stout, clean shaven and bald apart from a ridge of tufty hair above his ears and round the back of his head. He invariably wore T-shirts and jeans and a knitted woolly hat. He was good at his job and spent most of his spare time on car maintenance for his colleagues and neighbours.

His wife, Sylvia, was a local girl, a couple of years younger than him. She was of similar build and dressed just as casually. Her hair always looked as if it was waiting to be combed.

"No I haven't heard." she said, coming out of the kitchen, "Why? What's happened? How should I know what's going on at the depot?"

"Hasn't it been on the telly? One of our buses was held up by robbers this afternoon and the driver was shot dead."

"The telly's on the blink again, haven't had it on, I keep asking you to have it seen to. Who was shot? Anyone we know?"

"Pete Thompson, I don't know if you remember him, he hangs around a lot with that Stan Hollingsworth. They've both been at the depot much longer than I have."

"Pete Thompson was that strange bloke, wasn't he?" asked Sylvia, "The one who wouldn't dance with me at the do last Christmas. I didn't like him very much, his mate Stan was all right though."

"I don't know about that," replied Harry, "he seemed OK to me, although, apart from Stan, he didn't have any friends at the depot. He didn't mix with the lads or join in if anything was going on, kept himself to himself, if you know what I mean. Nobody deserves to die like that though. They were saying at the depot this afternoon that he had swapped shifts with Stan and shouldn't have been driving today. That's fate for you, I suppose. I shouldn't say it but if it had to happen I'm glad it was him and not Stan."

"Well, it's a nasty business but there's nothing anybody can do about it now." said Sylvia, "Come and have your tea before it gets cold, it's already on the table for you, and you can tell me all about it while you're eating."

As Stan Hollingsworth parked his car in its usual place at the bus garage and stepped out of it a small group of men standing beside a stationary bus stopped talking and looked towards him.

"Sorry about Pete!" one of them exclaimed as he approached them, "You've been mates for a long time."

"I don't really know what's happened yet." he replied "Freda saw it on television but missed most of it. I should have been on today, can't believe it!"

"You'd better go up to the office." said one of the group, "The police are there now, they can fill you in. We were just saying that this job is getting bloody dangerous; we ought to stick out for more money. What do you think?"

"I can't be bothered with things like that now." Hollingsworth replied. "All I can think about is Pete being dead, it should never have happened."

He made his way past the row of buses to the door at the back of the garage and rapidly climbed the stairs to the manager's office.

"Ah, Stan." said the depot manager as he entered the room. "Glad you're here, this is a sorry business believe me. In all my years in this job I've never known anything like it."

The manager turned to a man sitting by the desk and said to Stan, "This is Detective Inspector Harty of the C.I.D. who's taken over the case. We were just talking about you and he would like to ask you some questions."

To the Inspector he said, "This is Stan Hollingsworth, one of our drivers. He and Pete Thompson have been good friends for years. They've both been on the buses for about fifteen years, never a bad word between them."

"I want to know exactly what's happened!" exclaimed Stan. "Only saw it briefly on television. Why didn't anyone try to get in touch with me? It comes as a terrible shock when you see it like that."

"We've tried ringing you since about half past four." said the manager. "Kept getting the engaged signal. We were just about to send someone round to you when you came in."

"That perishing daughter of mine must have been on to her friends again." remarked Stan "Number of times I keep telling her about that but it doesn't make any difference. Keeps saying she wants a mobile but she's not getting one. Now tell me, what happened?"

Detective Inspector Harty related the whole story in detail.

"I understand that it was actually your shift." he added "and that Pete Thompson was filling in for you. Why weren't you at work today?"

"Had things to do at home. I'm in the middle of rebuilding our bathroom. My wife is fed up with the mess and keeps on to me to get it finished so Pete agreed to do my shift for me. The manager here OK'd it."

The manager nodded and said, "Yes, it was all right by me. As long as the job gets done I don't mind a little swapping around."

"When was this arranged?" asked the Inspector.

"On Sunday." said Hollingsworth, "I got quite a lot done over the weekend and Monday was a free day anyway so I thought if I had Tuesday off as well I could get most of the hard work finished."

"So, if you had been at work today it would have been you and not Pete Thompson lying in the morgue?"

"Yes, I suppose it would! Put like that it doesn't bear thinking about does it? I just can't believe that it has happened, it doesn't seem real somehow."

"What were you doing between two and three this afternoon?"

"Well, I was in the garden shed all afternoon making panels and cupboard doors. Finished dinner at about quarter past one and took a cup of tea out there with me. I had another cup of tea at about half past three, went back into the kitchen for it."

"Can anyone verify that you were in your shed at that time?"

"Freda, my wife can. Wait, surely you don't suspect me? Pete was my mate! We've been friends for years. What would I want to kill him for? And I'd hardly be likely to rob my own bus. Wouldn't know how to use a gun anyway".

"OK, calm down. We don't suspect anybody yet." said the Inspector. "We just have to tie up all the loose ends. We shall be asking that same question of many people in the next few days."

Stan sat with his head between his hands.

The manager said, "You'd better get off home, Stan. It's been a shock for all of us and especially you. Don't come in tomorrow if you don't feel up to it. I can get one of the lads to fill in."

Stan stood up, said "Thanks boss, I'll be all right." looked at the policeman and left the office.

As the door closed Detective Inspector Harty got up from his chair and said to the manager, "That's about all I can do for now. You will be seeing a lot more of me and my colleagues in the next few days, I'm afraid. This is a nasty business and we must get some answers quickly. If you hear, or come across anything that may help give the station a ring straight away. An incident room is being set up there and all calls should be put through to them."

He shook the manager's hand, left the office and made his way to his car and back to see how Sergeant Tully was progressing.

Chapter three

At ten o'clock the following morning, Wednesday, the passengers from the bus started to arrive at the police station to give their statements. A room had been set aside specially for the task and four detective constables were sitting at desks ready for the interviews. The job was being supervised by Detective Sergeant Tully.

"I shall interview the chap who had all that money taken," he said to them, "you four look after the others and make sure you get as much information as possible. If anything at all looks promising let me know straight away. Don't take too long over it though we don't want complaints from those who'll have to wait."

Turning to the people now seated on chairs provided for them at one end of the room he said "My men here will interview you individually and will ask you certain questions pertinent to the crime. Please give them as much information as you can but do keep within the facts. We won't keep you any longer than necessary but if any of you have urgent business please speak up and we will try to give you some priority. There is coffee and tea on that table in the corner, help yourselves while you're waiting and I thank you for your assistance. Mr Watkins, would you come over here please."

Mr Peter Watkins got up from his chair, walked across the room and accepted a seat at the Sergeant's side. He was a very average looking man, clean shaven, in his middle thirties, about five feet seven and wearing a brown sports jacket and brown trousers with a light chequered shirt and beige tie.

"Right Mr Watkins" said the Sergeant, "I believe you had about six thousand pounds or so taken yesterday, is that right?"

"Yes. To be exact there was five thousand eight hundred and forty pounds in takings from the shop and I had twenty pounds and fifty three pence of my own in my pocket. They also took my Barclaycard, my wristwatch and my mobile phone."

The Sergeant made a note of the amounts and then said "Is it your own shop?"

"No, I work in the newsagents in Wirral Road. I'm the manager there, been there over nine years now. We've had a couple of raids at the shop in the past but never on the way to the bank and have never lost as much as this before."

"Do you always go to the bank by bus?"

"Have done for the last four years or so. I used to go by car but parking's a big problem there now and it seemed safer by bus anyway. Always has been up to now, the bus stops right outside the bank and I catch it about fifty yards or so from the shop so I'm never in the street for very long with all that money on me."

"Do you always go by the same bus?"

"No, I go to the bank once a week, sometimes on Tuesdays and other times on Wednesdays. Can be morning or afternoon depending on how busy we are."

"Could it be that over the past few weeks you've caught the same bus on a Tuesday afternoon?"

"I don't think so. It's a bit difficult to remember clearly, it's a hectic business running a busy newsagents, you know. Things do tend to become a habit I know so I suppose it could be, but I don't think so."

"I'd be grateful if you could give that point some serious thought Mr Watkins, perhaps your staff can remember. You can give us a ring when you're clearer about it, it is important. Now, about the other passengers, can you tell me anything about them?"

One of the constables came across at this point and said "Sarge, it seems that two of the women passengers got on the bus at the same time as the gunmen, Mrs Talbot and Mrs Legge over there, thought you'd like to see them yourself."

"Yes I certainly would." said Detective Sergeant Tully. "Give them some tea while I finish with Mr Watkins. Tell them I won't be too long."

Turning again to Peter Watkins he said "Sorry about that. Now, can you tell me anything about the other passengers?"

"What sort of thing do you want to know? I don't usually talk to people on buses."

"Are any of them familiar to you? Is there any way they could know you were taking money to the bank?"

"I don't recognise anyone here today except from being on the bus with them yesterday. I suppose it's possible that one or more of them have been in the shop and seen me there. We get so many people in the shop that we tend not to notice them, if you know what I mean. Apart from the regulars, who mostly come in for their papers and cigarettes first thing in the morning, I couldn't really recognise anybody. As for the money for the bank I always carry that in a special bag strapped to my waist under my coat so I don't see how anybody can know I'm going to the bank."

"You did say that the bus stops outside the bank." said the Sergeant. "I expect you walk straight in from the bus. It wouldn't be difficult for someone to follow you in there and see what you're doing."

"That's never occurred to me, I must admit!" exclaimed Peter Watkins, a look of alarm crossing his face. "It just goes to show however careful you are there's always somewhere you slip up."

"Do you think that you have seen any one of these people on one of your earlier trips?"

"I'm afraid I can't say for sure, I don't really look at faces. I usually read or look out of the window. Some faces you feel sure you have seen before but can't remember where. Don't forget, as I've already said, we have a lot of people coming in and out of the shop."

"Don't worry, Mr Watkins, just one more question, was there anything familiar at all about any of the gunmen? Anything in their actions or about their person that rang a bell?"

"I only saw the two on the upper deck and I didn't recognise anything about them. They were young; I could tell that from the little of their faces I could see. They were scared too; you could see it in their eyes. In their late teens I should think, certainly wouldn't say they were older than twenty. By the way, that's something else I should mention, sometimes I travelled upstairs and sometimes down."

"Thank you very much Mr Watkins, you've been very helpful. Don't forget to let us know about your bus trips. Try to remember over the last two months or so when you travelled on Tuesdays and Wednesdays, and at what time of day. If anything else comes to mind as well be sure to tell us immediately. However unimportant it may seem to you it could be a vital piece of the jigsaw, so please bear that in mind. You're OK to go now."

As Peter Watkins left the room Detective Sergeant Tully went over to where Mrs Talbot and Mrs Legge were sitting, talking together, and pulled up a chair to sit facing them.

"Good morning ladies." he said "I won't keep you for very much longer. I understand that you boarded the bus yesterday afternoon at the same time as the raiders."

"Yes!" exclaimed the two women in Unison.

"You may be able to give us some positive information that will enable us to identify them. Will you please tell me all you can about them, and about their car, if possible?"

Mrs Talbot was the first to speak. She was a well-dressed woman of about forty-five wearing a fashionable beige raincoat with a large silk scarf over her shoulders, and an expensive looking hat. She was slim and obviously looked after herself. Her make-up was discreet and just enough to enhance her attractive features.

"I don't know about Mrs Legge" she said, "but I really didn't take a lot of notice. The men were already at the bus stop when we arrived. They were dressed in duffle coats, I think, and were huddled together talking. I think one of them was a lot older than the other three but I can't really be sure, I didn't see their faces clearly and, as I said, didn't take much notice. The bus came along as soon as we got to the shelter, I live in the house by the stop, you see, and wait until I see the bus turning the corner before I go out for it."

"While you were watching for the bus didn't you see the men arrive at the stop or perhaps the car pull up?" asked the Sergeant.

"No, I can't actually see the bus stop from the house because of the hedge. It is the top of the bus that comes into view over the neighbours' hedges. As for the car I didn't notice that at all, did you Alice?"

Alice Legge was not at all like her friend. She was about the same age but was quite plump and did not take nearly as much care of herself. She wore a short coat over a floral dress and a small, but quite attractive, hat. There was little evidence of make up on her face but it was a happy face and it was apparent that she didn't let things worry her too much.

"I did see a couple of cars parked down the road as we came out of your gate, Sophie, but couldn't tell you what they were or even their colour. To me they are just metal boxes on wheels."

Then addressing herself to Detective Sergeant Tully she continued "I thought it was unusual for those men to be at the bus stop though, it's normally empty at that time of day, but, like Sophie, I didn't take a lot of notice. The bus was almost there by then and I was mostly looking at that."

"Did you think, like Mrs Talbot here, that one of the men was older than the others?" asked the Sergeant.

"I didn't really give it any thought but when we were on the bus the one who did the shooting was definitely a lot older than the one who robbed us. While he was taking my money I thought how young he looked although most of his face was covered with a scarf. He had young looking eyes, you know, no more than a teenager I'd say. I'll tell you one thing, he looked very scared. If the circumstances had been different I could have felt quite sorry for him, but with that gun in his hand, well!"

"Do you catch the same bus regularly?" interrupted Sergeant Tully.

"Yes." said Sophie Talbot, "Alice comes over to me every Tuesday after lunch, she lives across the road, and we have a cup of tea and a chat then we catch the half-past two bus to the shops. That gives us plenty of time to get back by five before our husbands get home from work."

"Do you see the same people on the bus each week?"

"One gentleman and three of the women are usually on it although not always." she replied. "We say hello to them but that's all, we never talk to them so we don't really

22

know them at all. We always travel downstairs so don't know who's on the upper deck."

"Was anybody missing yesterday who is usually there?"

"Can't think of anybody, can you Alice? Mind you we're normally talking to each other and don't really look at the other passengers all that much."

"Sometimes there's a man sitting on the back seat." replied Alice. "He wasn't there yesterday."

"Can you describe him?" asked the Sergeant.

"About fortyish, wears a trilby and a raincoat, got a moustache. Should think he's fairly tall but I only see him sitting down."

"Did you notice the gentleman I was talking to just now?" asked the Sergeant. "Have you seen him on the bus before?"

"I don't think so, do you, Alice?" said Mrs Talbot.

Alice Legge shrugged and shook her head. "You must think us very unobservant, Sergeant." she said. "A couple of silly old gossip mongers."

"Not at all ladies, you've both been very helpful. If you think of anything else that may be of use please ring us here and let us know. Thank you Mrs Talbot, thank you Mrs Legge, I hope I haven't kept you too long, you're free to go whenever you wish."

All the interviews were over by twelve thirty when Detective Inspector Harty walked into the room. He asked Detective Sergeant Tully how it had gone.

"The total haul, excluding the fares and money taken from the bus driver, which we don't know about yet, amounts to about six thou sand six hundred pounds plus jewellery, credit cards and mobile phones. The jewellery is mostly necklaces, earrings and wrist watches, nothing of any great value. From what Mr Watkins, the newsagent, said nobody could be certain that he would be on that bus so it seems they were lucky to get as much as they did."

"Unless someone got a message to them that he would be there." said the Inspector, "They may have had a mobile 'phone in the car, wish we could get some information on that. Any joy on the four gangsters?"

"It seems pretty certain that the killer is between thirty and forty and the other three are all under twenty. Nothing about them was at all familiar to any of the passengers. They were all wearing duffle coats and used scarves to mask their faces. It was the eyes that gave away their ages, none of them said very much."

"I still favour someone on the buses, or at least linked with them in some way." the Inspector remarked, "Come on Bob; I think we'll have another word with Stan Hollingsworth."

Chapter four

Number sixteen Berwick Road was a three bedroom, semi-detached house built during the nineteen fifties. It had bay windows upstairs and down and all the woodwork had obviously recently been painted. It had a small but neat front garden with a well-kept lawn and colourful flower beds round the edges full of spring and early summer blossom. The garden was surrounded by a waist high red brick wall with a newly painted wrought iron gate giving entry to a path of crazy paving leading up to the porch and front door. Detective Inspector Harty pressed the bell push and gazed appreciatively around the garden while he waited for an answer.

"Mr Hollingsworth certainly seems keen on DIY." he said to Detective Sergeant Tully. "This all looks very nice."

The door was opened by Freda Hollingsworth who looked at the two plain clothed policemen enquiringly.

"Good afternoon," said the Inspector, showing his warrant card, "I am Detective Inspector Harty of West Town CID and this is Detective Sergeant Tully. Is Mr Hollingsworth there please?"

Freda Hollingsworth was an attractive thirty-eight year old brunette. Her hair was shoulder length with a slight curl and she was wearing a white blouse with red skirt covered by a frilly apron and had fancy slippers on her stockinged feet. She gave the impression of having a happy and leisurely life.

"No, I'm sorry, he's gone to work" she said, "aren't you the policeman he saw yesterday? He told me about you when he came home. It's awful what happened to

Pete. Stan said that you seem to think he's involved in it somehow, but that's daft."

"Yes, I did have a few words with him yesterday but I told him then that nobody is under suspicion yet. We have to start somewhere and Thompson was working his shift, however there are a few more questions I would like to ask."

"He won't be home until about six o'clock and he'll be out on his bus now, I shudder every time I think that he should have been on it yesterday. I wish he hadn't gone in today, his boss told him he needn't, but, as Stan said, the same thing's hardly likely to happen again today."

"I should certainly hope not." the Inspector said, but not to worry, we'll catch him later. Do you mind if we come in and ask you some questions?"

"Me? Yes, I suppose so. You can come in but I don't know if I can be of much help to you."

As they entered the hall and the front door was closed behind them Detective Inspector Harty noticed that the television was on in the kitchen. Freda escorted them into the lounge and invited them to take a seat.

"You have a very nice place here, Mrs Hollingsworth," said Inspector Harty. "It's a credit to you and your husband."

"Yes, Stan is always making improvements, he's not one to sit around and do nothing. Would you like a cup of tea? I was just about to pour one for myself."

They sat on the settee and accepted her offer of tea. During the few moments she was out of the room their eyes wandered over its contents hoping to get some idea of the Hollingsworth's life style. She returned with a trolley carrying three cups of tea, a bowl of sugar and a plate of biscuits.

The Inspector said. "Your husband tells me he's refurbishing your bathroom, not the easiest of jobs I should think."

"Yes, he's nearly finished it now. It looks very nice but it has taken a long time. I'm afraid I've been on to him quite a bit to get it finished. The trouble is he tries to do too many jobs at the same time, he interrupted the job on the bathroom in order to paint the outside of the house while the weather was nice."

"It must be very inconvenient having the bathroom in a mess, I know my wife wouldn't tolerate it for long. Mr Hollingsworth said that he was in the shed all yesterday afternoon making panels and things, can you confirm that?"

"Oh yes, he went out there at about quarter past one, after lunch, and came back in at about half past four, when Claire, our daughter, came home from school."

"And he didn't leave it or go out at all during that time?"

"He came in at half past three for a cup of tea but the rest of the time he was out there. Why are you asking these questions?"

"Just routine, I assure you. We must be certain of everybody's movements yesterday afternoon. Are you sure that he couldn't have gone out without you knowing? What were you doing yourself?"

"I was in the kitchen watching the afternoon soaps on television, I always watch those, Stan says I'm addicted. He wouldn't have gone out without telling me first, he would have come through the kitchen anyway."

"Do you mind if Detective Sergeant Tully has a look in the garden shed?"

"By all means, we've nothing to hide, but please don't touch anything, Stan is fussy about his tools."

The Sergeant left the room and went through the kitchen into the garden while the Inspector continued to ask questions of Freda Hollingsworth.

"What can you tell me about Pete Thompson, the driver who was shot? He and your husband were good friends weren't they?"

"Yes, Stan met Pete when he went for the interview for the job on the buses, about fifteen years ago now, I think. They both got the jobs at the same time and have been close friends ever since."

"As far as we can determine Mr Thompson had no relatives, is that right?"

"Not quite, he has a cousin who lives nearby, they're not very close but he visits them, sorry, used to visit, fairly frequently, I believe. He was an only child and his mum and dad died some time ago. They had him quite late in life, didn't think they would have any kids until he arrived apparently. They doted on him. His Aunt and Uncle, the cousin's parents, are dead as well I believe."

"You said he visited them, I take it the cousin is married. Is the cousin male or female?"

"Oh sorry, male. He is married and has a daughter, Kerry, she's about the same age as our daughter Claire, fourteen. Pete has brought her round here once or twice, quite a pretty girl. I've never met the cousin or his wife and don't know much about them, Stan can tell you more. The cousin's name is Geoff, I don't know the surname."

"Can you give me his address?"

"No, I don't know it, but I'm sure Stan can tell you. I think he's been round there once or twice with Pete."

"Was Mr Thompson a bachelor?"

"He was married when we first knew him but it wasn't a happy marriage, they were always arguing. His wife, Sarah, divorced him about ten years ago. I think his mother's influence was behind it, it's a shame but it often seems to happen to an only child, especially a boy, doesn't it?. They didn't have any children thank goodness. She remarried and moved away somewhere, I don't think he heard any more from her."

"What about lady friends? Did he have many relationships?"

"Pete was a strange man, as far as I know he's had no girlfriends at all since his wife left him. He always said they didn't interest him. He had a computer at home and spent a lot of his spare time on that, and a lot of his money I think. I've never seen it, haven't been to his place, so don't know what he did with it. The rest of his spare time seems to have been spent with Stan or visiting his cousin."

Detective Sergeant Tully came through the door into the lounge at that moment and said that everything in the shed was as it should be.

"What did Mr Thompson and your husband do when they were together?" the Inspector asked Mrs Hollingsworth.

"Well, Pete used to help Stan with whatever job he was doing. He was nothing like as good as Stan was with his hands, though. It often surprised me how Stan put up with him, he must have been more of a hindrance than a help. I never once saw Stan get angry with him although he looked annoyed more than once. Mind you, Pete was good at gardening and Stan was glad when he could give him something to do out there."

"Do I understand from that that Mr Thompson was an unwelcome visitor?"

"Oh no, although there were days when we both wished he had stayed away. Stan felt sorry for him, I think, because he was so lonely. He never mixed with anybody you see. I suppose it was all to do with his background. I just tried to pretend he wasn't there most of the time.

The Inspector said "You have been very helpful Mrs Hollingsworth, thank you. You have told us most of the things we needed to know. There are one or two points we still want clarified by your husband and would like to do that this evening when he returns from work. What time would be convenient? It shouldn't take long."

"Any time after six thirty would be all right. I'll let him know you're coming as soon as he gets in."

The Inspector and Sergeant left the house and as Freda was about to close the door the Inspector said "Oh, would you ask your husband to write down the address of Mr Thompson's cousin for me?"

As they sat in the car outside the house before driving off Detective Sergeant Tully said "Well, the shed has certainly been used recently for woodwork and there's no reason to doubt that he was there all yesterday afternoon but the shed is hidden from the house by a couple of large bushes. He could have slipped away down the side of the house while his missus was watching her soaps. You know what women are like when they get engrossed in them and they are on almost non-stop from one thirty to three thirty. Plenty of time to do the job and get back for his cup of tea."

"Perhaps, but why would he do it? I don't think he's hard up enough to want to rob a bus load of passengers, and then share it four ways. From the look of the house they are quite comfortable. Of course it could have been done just for the thrill, stranger things have happened, and possibly Pete Thompson recognised him and had to be put out of the way. But this is all conjecture, nothing at all concrete. At the moment Stan Hollingsworth is the most likely suspect, in fact the only one, and he did jump very rapidly to the conclusion that we suspected him, but we must keep an open mind."

"Maybe Pete Thompson was having it off with his wife" said the Sergeant "she's a very nice bit of stuff, and Hollingsworth found out and decided to kill two birds with one stone."

"From what she told me while you were outside Bob, that just won't wash. Of course, at the moment we've only got her word for it, but Thompson wasn't interested in women. In any case, from the way she spoke, I don't think she had too much time for Pete Thompson. Perhaps things will become a little clearer when we talk to Mr Hollingsworth this evening."

With that DS Tully started the car and they headed back to West Town.

Chapter five

Detective Inspector Harty and Detective Sergeant Tully were sitting together in the incident room at West Town police station comparing notes.

"We haven't made a lot of progress," said the Inspector "there are no leads so far as to who the robbers might be, but it's early days yet. I rather think that things will start to crawl out of the woodwork before very much longer. A robbery like this involving four men is bound to lead to a disagreement of some sort."

"It seems pretty certain that three of them are hardly men." remarked Sergeant Tully. "To use teenagers like that and with guns is unusual to say the least. The killer must be pretty sure of himself and must have some sort of control over those lads otherwise one of them, at least, would have come out into the open by now. They must be pretty panic stricken, I should think, or as hard as nails!"

"Yes, I've been giving that a lot of thought. Who are they and where do they come from? If we could get some idea of that it could, perhaps, give us the key to the whole thing. Are you sure that none of the passengers you saw this morning could give us any information at all that would help to identify them?"

"Yes, I am guv! They were all too startled and worried about their own safety to notice or remember much, and, as you said yourself, weren't very observant anyway. We know that all the gunmen were wearing duffle coats or anoraks and that they all had dark scarves covering their faces. A couple of the passengers on the upper deck said that they thought one of the youths had fair hair, oh! And the one taking the money downstairs was wearing a new pair of trainers. Not much to go on."

At that moment a uniformed sergeant opened the door and entered the room. He walked across to Detective Inspector Harty.

"A burnt out car was found on the old derelict railway sidings this morning, Inspector." he said. "There was a body in the driving seat, impossible to identify. It was thought at first to be a suicide but forensic found this among the ashes and are wondering if it's anything to do with your case. Of course, it could belong to the corpse anyway but it needs checking out."

He handed the Inspector a gold earring. The Inspector turned it over in his hand then gave it to Sergeant Tully.

"Get DC Robson to check that with the passengers who lost earrings yesterday. We'll go and have a look at the car, tell Robson to meet us there when he's finished."

When they arrived at the old sidings the scene of crime officer took them to see Inspector Harriot of the forensic squad who was kneeling by the burnt out shell of the car and studying the remains very closely.

"Whoever did this did a very thorough job." said Inspector Harriot. "It definitely wasn't suicide so it's very likely the car you are looking for. The whole vehicle must have been swamped with petrol and then ignited. We found a couple of empty petrol cans over there and are checking them for finger prints. The cans were quite new, couldn't have been here long, may even have come from the boot of the car. From what we can see so far the boot and the glove compartment were completely empty before the fire so there would have been nothing to help us there anyway. The registration plates hadn't been removed but they were plastic and there's very little left of them so we still have no idea of the vehicle number. We might be able to get something from the engine number but that's going to take a little while. The body's over there waiting to be taken away, Doctor Perry's still looking at it if you want to talk to him."

"Yes, thanks, I will." said Detective Inspector Harty, "I imagine the poor sod found in the car must have been already dead, or at least unconscious before the car was set alight, otherwise he'd hardly still be sitting in the driving seat. Where was the earring found?"

"Under the driving seat." said Inspector Harriot. "As you can see there's no upholstery left so it could have dropped from the victim's clothes, or his person, as they burned. It could, of course, already have been there."

"We'll know more about that when DC Robson returns." said Inspector Harty, "Meanwhile I'll have a chat with the Doctor. Oh! By the way, what make of car was it?"

"Vauxhall Astra, not the latest model, can't tell what colour it was, should know more when we get back to the lab."

"Who found it?"

"Two boys on their way to school this morning. They shouldn't have been here, we are always telling them how dangerous it is, but they said they were late and were taking a short cut. If they hadn't been we probably wouldn't have found it, it could have been here for weeks."

"That's probably what the murderer was banking on. Hopefully it may be a lucky break for us. Didn't anyone see the fire?"

"A fire was noticed from the houses over the other side of the site on Tuesday afternoon but they just thought it was rubbish being burnt, that's happened before. They only saw the smoke, as you can see this part of the site is pretty well hidden. It looks as though the Doctor's getting ready to go you'd better get over to him."

"The body's too badly burned to tell you much here Inspector." said Dr Perry as Inspector Harty approached. "I'll be able to tell you more once I've carried out the post-mortem. There's hardly any flesh left. At the moment I can't say for sure if it's male, but I think it is. I can't tell you yet how he died either."

"So you have no idea yet about how old he was?"

"No, but, if it's of any use, the feet suffered slightly less than the rest of the body and it looks as though he was wearing trainers. There's not much left of them but I'm sure they're men's."

"He could be the boy on the lower deck of the bus, a couple of passengers noticed he had new trainers." said the Inspector, "I very much doubt that it was the man who shot the bus driver."

Detective Constable Robson arrived at that moment and said "It's definitely our case Guv, that earring belongs to Mrs Talbot . She recognised it as soon as I showed it to her. It was bought for her by her husband on her last birthday apparently."

"Well Doctor," said Inspector Harty, "It doesn't look as though there's much doubt that this is one of the robbers, and that is probably the car they used to get away from the scene. If you can tell me all you can about the body as soon as possible I'd be very grateful. We might be able to identify him from our records, you never know, then we might start getting somewhere."

"Bob," he called, "We'd better be going to see Hollingsworth, the meeting with him is even more important now. Have you managed to learn anything here?"

"Yes Guv. The forensic boys found the remains of a gun in the car but it wasn't a real one, it was a replica. It's beginning to look as though the killer was probably the only one with a real gun."

"That makes sense." replied the Inspector. "I wasn't happy with a man like that letting youngsters have guns, no telling what they'd do. He's thought this thing through all right. Now I wonder if this boy's death was intentional or not. If it was I don't hold out much hope for the other two. It could be though that this one knew too much because of the shooting on the bus. Everything at the moment points to him being the second robber downstairs, the two upstairs couldn't have known what was going on. Mrs Talbot's earring and the trainers seem to confirm that. If the gunman was going to kill them all he could have done it at the same time and left them all in the car."

"Probably what I said yesterday." remarked the Sergeant. "Wants all the loot to himself, greedy. That's why he used teenagers, they don't have any experience and are easier to get rid of."

"You could be right but what has happened to the other two?. I wonder if they are still alive and, if they are, are they locked up somewhere? They must be scared silly. It's a bit early yet but tomorrow we can start checking the missing persons list for teenage boys, someone should have missed at least one of them by now I should think. It may give us some pointers."

"Somehow I doubt that," said Detective Sergeant Tully, "they're probably layabouts who won't be missed for weeks. Robson! You get back to the station and type up your report on that earring."

The Detective Inspector and Sergeant got into their car and headed once more for Berwick Road and Stan Hollingsworth.

"Oh, hello Inspector." said Stan Hollingsworth as he answered the front door and stood to one side, "Come on in. Freda told me you were coming but I expected you a little earlier than this."

"Yes," replied Detective Inspector Harty stepping into the hall, "something else came up but it's important we speak to you tonight, by the way this is Detective Sergeant Tully."

Stan Hollingsworth was a stocky man who obviously enjoyed a pint or two, probably of lager. Forty years of age, he was clean shaven and had a thick, unruly mop of hair. His brown eyes constantly moved from one to the other of the visitors. The green sweater and brown corduroy trousers he was wearing made him look shorter than his five feet nine inches. He nodded to the Sergeant and ushered them both into the lounge where Freda was sitting.

"Sorry to come back so late Mrs Hollingsworth but there were fresh developments this afternoon. It's more important than ever that we speak to your husband." said the Inspector, "A cup of tea would be nice if you wouldn't mind please."

As Freda left the room the Inspector turned to Stan Hollingsworth and asked "Do you own a car sir?"

"Yes, it's parked out front, you must have seen it, a red Ford Fiesta, had it about eighteen months now."

"Does your wife have a car?"

"No, she can't drive, never wanted to, even if she could we couldn't afford two cars on my pay."

"Does your wife have a job?"

"No, she hasn't worked since Claire was born, never really needed to. A bus driver's pay isn't the earth but it's not all that bad really, especially with overtime and there's plenty of that, enough for us to live on without Freda having to work too. Anyway, why all these questions about Freda? Where does she fit into all this?"

"Just background sir, nothing to worry about. Now, your friendship with the murdered driver can you tell me more about that?"

"What sort of thing do you want to know?"

"How often did you see him? What did you do together? Your wife told me that he avoided female relationships and only occasionally saw his cousin, what did he do when he was not with you?"

"Oh yes, you wanted his cousin's address. Here it is." said Stan Hollingsworth taking a piece of paper from his trouser pocket and handing it to the Inspector. "Well, he used to come round here three or four times a week, sometimes during the day, sometimes of an evening, depending on how our shifts worked out. During the day he would help me with a bit of DIY or gardening, of an evening we would watch television or play cards or go to the pub, whichever took our fancy, he was really just like one of the family."

"What did your wife do while he was here with you? Didn't she resent it?"

"Who, Freda? No she enjoyed his company as much as I did, didn't you love?" he directed at his wife as she entered the room carrying a tray. "Pete was a good bloke to have around, we shall miss him."

"What did he do when he wasn't with you?"

"He'd visit his cousin Geoff's place about once a fortnight and sometimes took Kerry, Geoff's daughter, out somewhere. He took our Claire out a few times as well, that was the sort of bloke he was. Most of the rest of his spare time he spent at his own place on his computer, quite a good system he's got there, cost him a bomb. Don't know much about them myself and he liked to be alone when he was using it so I don't know what he used it for."

"Weren't you curious?" asked Detective Sergeant Tully. "You say you were close friends and yet he didn't want you there."

"I didn't say he didn't want me there, it's just that some things are like that. He said he couldn't concentrate when other people were around. I could understand that and I wasn't particularly interested in the computer myself anyway. All right, they're clever things I suppose but I could never understand what people see in them, much prefer a good football match or a film on television."

"What can you tell us about this cousin of his?" asked the Inspector.

"Geoff Matthews? Oh, he seems a decent enough fellow. I've only met him a couple of times so don't know him too well. He's a bit older than Pete, about forty-five I should say. His wife, Mary, is a nice little thing and he dotes on his daughter, Kerry, she's about the same age as our Claire. He works for British Gas, I believe, as a central heating maintenance engineer. According to Pete he's been with them since he left school."

"Do you know if Mr Thompson had any other friends?"

"Pete was a loner, don't really know why he latched on to me although I suppose it was because we both started on the buses on the same day and there was some kinship there. No, he didn't make friends, in fact he wasn't very popular at the depot. Most of the lads thought he was toffee nosed but I think it was shyness more than anything. The only other person I've really known him to talk to at the depot was one of the maintenance crew, Harry Davies, but I wouldn't call it friendship. Harry always started the conversation and Pete wouldn't have wanted to ignore him. As far as I know that's as far as it went.

"Just one more question Mr Hollingsworth, and we'll be on our way. What make of car did Mr Thompson have and do you know where it is?"

"A Vauxhall Astra, about five years old. I should imagine it's in the car park at the depot. Pete always used it to go to work and he didn't get back there to drive it home, did he?"

"Thank you Mr Hollingsworth that's all for now but it's possible we may want to speak to you again. Thanks for the tea Mrs Hollingsworth, we'll see ourselves out."

Once outside he said to the Sergeant "Has anyone been round to the murdered driver's house, Bob?"

"Yes but not yet for a detailed look."

"First thing tomorrow send a couple of the lads round there to see if they can find anything that may help, and get someone who knows their way round computers. I'd be interested to know what he did on that thing. Let's call it a day, it's been a very long one. I think we both need a good meal and some sleep."

Chapter six

At number nine, Thirston Close, Geoff Matthews was sitting at the kitchen table while his wife, Mary, cooked his usual breakfast of sausage, bacon and egg. It was eight thirty on Thursday morning and he had just arrived home from his night shift with the emergency service of the gas company.

He was a fairly heavily built man, forty-three years of age, with broad hands which showed clearly that he was used to hard work. His rugged face and blue eyes gave a strong hint of good humour while his hair, already greying, was beginning to recede from his forehead.

Mary, by contrast, was a petite creature barely five feet tall, her dark hair was neatly curled and framed a rather plain face which did little to belie her thirty-eight years. She felt comfortable in her marriage to Geoff and this was reflected in the careless way she dressed, everything clean but nothing matched.

The house was neat and spotless with everything in its place. The furniture was not expensive but was kept in tiptop condition. The house and its contents were Mary's pride and joy and she constantly fussed around making sure that everything was just as it should be. Her husband was well used to this and took little notice, he had given up years before trying to change her ways, but it was rather off putting to visitors with the result that people seldom called.

This did not matter to either of them as they were not a particularly social pair, both much preferring their own company to that of outsiders and determined that their only child, Kerry, should have everything that they had been denied in their own childhood. They were clearly very much in love with each other and lived in a world of their own. They both adored Kerry but were determined not to spoil her and allowed her freedom to develop her own lifestyle while quietly making sure that she obeyed certain rules. They had both wanted more than the one child but this was not to be.

"'fraid you've missed Kerry this morning Geoff." said Mary, "She's already gone to school, some project they're working on, to do with improving the environment I think."

"That's a shame, I look forward to seeing our little princess when I get home." said Geoff as he unfolded the local newspaper he had bought on the way home. "Never mind I'll see her later. Hey, they didn't waste time getting Pete's murder on the front page." he said. "The whole page is taken up with the robbery and the way Pete was killed."

"Well, it's a very nasty business." replied Mary, "I don't think I'll ever get over Pete getting shot like that and all for nothing I'll bet. Fancy holding up a bus of all things, what did they hope to get? "

"According to this they got over six thousand quid plus some credit cards."

"Still not worth killing anyone for, especially Pete. I know we weren't all that close but he was your cousin. I always thought he was a very nice man, very quiet and unassuming. Our Kerry's going to miss him, he's taken her out quite a few times lately. I thought that was good of him, he didn't have to."

"I was talking to the manager in the newsagents round the corner this morning." said Geoff. "Do you know, he was on that bus, he was on his way to the bank and they took his week's takings, must have made up most of the loot. Makes you wonder if they knew he was going to be there."

"Oh, that must have been a nasty shock for him, you wouldn't expect something like that to happen on a local bus. Did he see Pete killed?"

"No, apparently he was on the top deck. He heard three shots downstairs but doesn't know which one killed Pete although he thinks it was probably the last one. The two men who held him up had gone down before the last shot was fired but he couldn't get to the stairs for other people in the way. He doesn't know which of the four robbers fired the shot at Pete but he seems pretty certain it wasn't either of the two who robbed him. He reckons they were only kids."

"Kids! I really don't know what the world's coming to. What makes them do things like that?" said Mary, "I bet that newsagent won't take his money to the bank by bus again."

"Oh, he's not worried, it must be covered by insurance. It's not his money anyway. No, he's got a story he can tell over and over again. Wouldn't surprise me if he makes some money out of it from the newspapers."

"That shouldn't be allowed!" retorted Mary, "Making money out of other peoples grief isn't very nice."

"I'm not getting into that sort of argument." said Geoff, wiping the last vestige of egg from his plate with a piece of bread, "I'm going upstairs for a bit of shut-eye, there are one or two things I want to do before I go to work tonight."

He bent down to give Mary a kiss. "Give me a call at about two o'clock if I'm not awake, love."

He had been in bed barely ten minutes when there was a knock at the front door. Mary answered it and found two men standing there.

"Mrs Matthews?" asked the one nearer the door. "I am Detective Inspector Harty of West Town C.I.D. and this is Detective Sergeant Tully. Is Mr Matthews at home?"

"He is but he has just gone to bed, he has been on night work and has not long been home."

"Could we see him please, we would like to ask one or two questions about the incident on Tuesday which involved his cousin, Mr Thompson."

"Can't it wait until later? He's had a busy night and is probably asleep by now. I don't suppose he can tell you anything you don't know already."

"I'm sorry, madam, it won't take long and it's very important that we get as much information as possible quickly if we want to catch the culprits."

"He won't like being disturbed. I don't know how he can help you, he wasn't there. It's not going to help Pete now anyway, is it?"

"We have to cover every avenue, Mrs Matthews, I'm sorry but I would appreciate it if you would please call him."

"You had better come in then, wait here while I get him."

Mary ushered them into the lounge then went upstairs.

After a few minutes Geoff Matthews entered the room bleary eyed saying "Couldn't this have waited until this afternoon? Mary told you I'd been on nights. I'd just gone into a deep sleep, don't suppose I'll get any sleep today now that I've been interrupted."

"I'm sorry sir, but there are a few questions I need to ask you to help in our investigation. I'll try not to keep you from your bed for too long. Mr Peter Thompson was your cousin, I understand."

"Yes."

"How well did you know him? I believe he called round here to see you quite frequently?"

"Well, he came round here about once a fortnight and stayed for a couple of hours or so, didn't really know him all that well even though he was my cousin, tended to keep himself to himself. Sometimes he'd come round to take Kerry, our daughter, out somewhere. Apart from that he spent most of his time on that computer of his. Lonely sort of bloke, if you know what I mean. He had a friend though, Stan Hollingsworth, one of the drivers he worked with on the buses. He probably knew Pete more than I did. Why don't you speak to him?"

"I already have, Mr Matthews. Do you know what your cousin did on his computer?"

"No idea. Wasn't interested, give me a good film any day, don't know what people see in computers, boring if you ask me. I get enough having to use one for work without having one at home. All right for kids I suppose."

"OK. Was he related to you on your father or mother's side?"

"What on earth has that got to do with anything? He was my father's brother's son if you must know."

"Do you have a car, Mr Matthews?"

"Yes, it's in the garage, I have the firm's van while I'm on call. That's parked out front."

"What make and colour is the car?"

"It's a blue and black Ford Focus, nearly two years old, had it from new."

"Does your wife have a car?"

"No. She uses the Focus when she needs to."

"One last question then you can get back to bed. Where were you between one and four pm on Tuesday afternoon?"

"I went into town to buy some trousers."

"Can anybody verify that?"

"We both went." said Mary. "We always go into town together."

"Did you go by car or bus?"

"That's three questions you've asked already." remarked Geoff Matthews. "We went by car and parked in the multi-story car park by the station. Now can I go back to bed?"

"Thank you sir. I'm sorry you had to be disturbed." said the Inspector, "That will be all for now but I may need to see you again."

"Well, try to make it when I'm not in bed." said Matthews as he saw them out of the house and closed the door behind them.

"He could have been a bit more co-operative." remarked Sergeant Tully as they walked towards their car. "After all it's his cousin's murder we're investigating."

"Can't say that I blame him" replied the Inspector, "we know ourselves what it's like to be called out of bed at short notice. I'd like you to check the hairdressers in town, Bob, start near the station, Mrs Matthews has recently had her hair done. I'd like to know when."

"I'd noticed that too. It usually takes a couple of hours in those places in which case he could have been on his own that afternoon. Of course, she could have had it done at home."

"Possibly, but unlikely I'd say. By the way did you find someone to have a look at Thompson's computer system?"

"Yes, apparently DC Robson is quite knowledgeable. He and WPC Jenny Wright should be round there now looking at that and anything else of interest."

"Good, we'll leave them to it and hear what they have to report later. Let's make our way to the mortuary. Dr Perry should have some news for us by now from the post-mortem. On the way there we can stop off at the bus depot to check on Thompson's car."

Arriving at the bus depot they called in at the manager's office.

"Good morning Inspector," he said, "Hope you have some news for us, the lads are getting a bit restless. An incident like this is very unsettling you know. They're all eyeing everybody at bus stops with suspicion."

"Oh, I doubt whether it'll happen again, not yet anyway, although, of course, until we know who did it and why nobody can be sure. No, we have nothing for you yet, the reason we are here is to check on the dead driver's car. Is it still in the car park?"

"Quite honestly I don't know, must admit it hadn't occurred to me, too many other things on my mind. Nobody else has mentioned it either, we'd better go and have a look."

The manager took them out to a walled area at the back of the maintenance area where several cars were parked.

"This is where it should be." he said, "Let's see, Pete had an Astra, that looks like it over there."

He took them over to a blue Vauxhall Astra backed up to the wall and opened the driver's door. The ignition key was in place.

"Don't they lock their cars?" asked Sergeant Tully

"No," replied the manager, "they're perfectly safe here and we ask the men to leave their keys with the cars in case they have to be moved while they're out on the buses."

"Can you confirm absolutely that this is Mr Thompson's car?" asked the Inspector.

The manager opened the glove compartment and took out a plastic wallet which contained documents pertaining to the car and its owner. There was no doubt that this was indeed Peter Thompson's car.

"Do you want the car?" asked the manager.

"No, we just needed to confirm its whereabouts." said the Inspector. "You'd better inform Mr Matthews at 9, Thirston Close, he's Mr Thompson's next of kin. He'll take it off your hands. While we're here you have a maintenance man, a Mr Harry Davies, who seems to have been on speaking terms with Thompson. Do you mind if we have a few words with him?"

I'm afraid he's out on a job at the moment, Inspector." said the depot manager, "I can't tell you how long he's likely to be."

"Does he often work away from the depot?"

"Well, I shouldn't admit it I suppose but the buses do break down more frequently than we would like, most of them are due for replacement this year or next. Yes, he's usually called out once or twice nearly every day."

"Never mind, perhaps we can see him next time we're here. Well, thank you for your time, we'll let you know when we have something definite to put your drivers' minds at rest."

As they made their way back to their own car Detective Inspector Harty said to Detective Sergeant Tully "It obviously wasn't Thompson's car used in the robbery, another theory bites the dust. It looks as though we might have another suspect though in this chap Davies. I still have a gut feeling that somebody to do with the buses is involved and if he's out and about as much as we're told he is he could have had the opportunity. Find out, Bob, what he was doing and where he was supposed to be on Tuesday afternoon. We must have a chat with him as soon as we can. For now let's get over to Dr Perry and see what he has for us."

Chapter seven

As Detective Inspector Harty and Detective Sergeant Tully entered the mortuary Dr Perry came out of his office and walked over to meet them.

Dr Perry had been carrying out post-mortems and medical work for the police for over twenty years and was very good at his job. His painstaking approach had on several occasions found evidence which others might have missed and which had made a significant difference to the solving of a case. He was a meek mannered little man of five feet four inches but could stand his ground with the best if needs be. He was fifty-four years of age, of slim build which made him look taller than he was and, under his white coat, wore an immaculate suit, usually of navy blue. He had a good head of hair, not yet thinning, but with evidence of greying at the temples and sported a Clark Gable type moustache. He wore half lens spectacles which he habitually peered over when not working.

"Hello Ted" he said, "thought you'd be along about now. I'm just going for a cup of coffee, come and join me and I'll tell you what I've found."

The Inspector beckoned Sergeant Tully to follow and the three walked together down the corridor towards a vending machine standing in a corner.

"Hope you've found something useful that we can get to grips with." said the Inspector to Dr Perry. "So far nothing of any significance in this case has come to light. It's beginning to get rather frustrating."

"Well, I can tell you that it definitely wasn't an accident or suicide and that the lad was dead before the car was set alight. He was shot through the left temple, at close range, probably by someone sitting in the passenger seat beside him. I don't think there can be any doubt that he was shot while he was sitting at the steering wheel, it's extremely difficult, you know, to place a dead body in the driving seat of a car."

"You said 'he' so the corpse is male then as you suspected?"

"Yes, a young male, eighteen or nineteen years of age, may be a little younger but certainly no older."

"Did you find anything on him that may help to identify him?"

"As you saw yesterday, the corpse was extremely badly burned so the chance of finding any distinguishing marks was practically nil. There were no rings on the fingers or signs of any other jewellery he may have worn. I did, however, find signs of fillings in his teeth, not more than three years old I should say, and one top right molar was missing. I think your best bet would be to try to trace his dental records, if he's a local lad that shouldn't be too difficult."

"Let's hope he was local, we need something definite to go on quickly now before the trail gets too cold. Can you tell me anything about his height and build?"

"He must have been a fairly slim lad, caucasian, five feet nine inches without shoes, sorry I can't tell you the colour of his hair."

"Thank you Doctor." said the Inspector, "This should be a big help. If you can let me have the details necessary to trace his dental records I'll get that moving straight away. I must admit that I'm very worried about the fate of the other two youngsters involved. Perhaps, if we can identify this one quickly it will lead us to them. Somehow, though, I rather think that we are probably already too late, the man we're after doesn't seem to have any scruples. Let's hope I'm being too pessimistic."

The Doctor gave them the information they needed and said, "There are five dental practices in town. They have to keep detailed records of all their patients, as you no doubt know. It won't be difficult for them to check out this information."

"Come on Bob," the Inspector said, turning to Detective Sergeant Tully, "let's get back to the station and get this under way. We can tot up what information we have so far while we're waiting."

It took only a few minutes to get back to West Town police station and organise the dental search. As they entered the incident room DC Robson greeted them.

"Oh, Sarge," he said, addressing Detective Sergeant Tully, "Mr Watkins, the newsagent manager, 'phoned a short while ago with the information you wanted about his bus trips. Thinking back, and checking with his assistant, he's pretty sure that he must have gone to the bank on the same bus each Tuesday afternoon for the last four or five weeks at least, says he'll make sure he varies it in future, too late now, I'd say. He also says that he's certain he travelled on the top deck each time too, couldn't stand the nattering women downstairs."

"Thanks Frank." replied the Sergeant, "None of that surprises me. You weren't long at Thompson's place, have you finished looking at his computer?"

"Not yet Sarge, He's certainly got a nice set up there, latest high resolution multimedia job, gives top quality pictures on screen you know. It's got a five hundred gigabyte hard disk too and a twenty-two inch LCD screen. Must have cost him a few hundred pounds. There's wireless broadband as well so he must have been in touch with other users. The only things I've found on it so far are a few games including chess and backgammon, a golf simulator and a couple of flight simulators. There's also a word processor, a home accounts programme, a spreadsheet and two sophisticated art programmes. Nothing much there to get excited about but there is one partition on the disk that I haven't been able to get into, needs a password and you can't guess at a thing like that although I've given it a couple of tries. It won't let you carry on at all after the third attempt. I'm popping over to the college later on to see if they can give any tips. They have some real whizz kids over there."

"OK, you've done well. What about WPC Wright? Has she come up with anything?"

"She's still foraging about over there, there are stacks to get through. Tell you what, she found a porno video hiding under the title 'GREAT EXPECTATIONS by Charles Dickens' gave her quite a shock, it was very explicit."

"So! Our bus driver who didn't like women liked watching hard porn!" said Sergeant Tully, "Had a sense of humour too it seems. That's interesting, but I don't know where it gets us."

"Right Bob," said Detective Inspector Harty turning his attention to Sergeant Tully, "Let's sum up and see what we've got so far."

"From what we heard just now it seems pretty certain that someone knew that Mr Watkins was going to be on that bus and that he was going to the bank with the takings from the shop. That has got to be the motive for the robbery otherwise it would hardly be worthwhile. To hide that fact our robber hired three youths from somewhere, probably out of work louts hanging around the streets, or pubs, and kitted them out in similar coats and scarves to his own, gave each of them a replica handgun and staged the holdup of the whole bus. We know, from the passengers on the bus, and from the post-mortem, that the driver was shot in the hand before he was killed because he reached for something. I think he was probably going to try to shut the doors to trap them inside the bus. As it happens that could have been very dangerous for everyone there so perhaps it was just as well that he didn't succeed. We don't know why he was killed but, most likely, he recognised one of the robbers, presumably the one nearest to him, the older one, the one who did the shooting. There is very little doubt that this man also shot and killed the lad in the burnt out car. It could be that the lad was creating a fuss about the shooting of the driver and threatened to tell the police, therefore had to be put out of the way, or perhaps the killer is getting rid of witnesses who can point the finger at him, in which case, the other two are probably already dead. The question here is, where were they when the first lad was shot and where are they now?"

"I checked the missing persons list first thing this morning." said Sergeant Tully. "There was no one reported who would fit the bill for any of the three we are looking for."

"They could be, as I said, three out of work louts who have either left home or been chucked out by their parents," replied the Inspector, "in which case they may not be missed for some time. Our best hope there is for the dental information Dr Perry has given us to quickly identify the dead lad. Probably once we have that we shall also know who the other two are. Now, for suspects, so far we have three, Stan Hollingsworth, Geoff Matthews, and the maintenance engineer Harry Davies who we still need to check out. The only reason, so far, that they are suspect is because we know that they knew Thompson and could have been recognised by him, but the same thing can be said for anyone working at the bus garage, we must interview them all. From what we have seen of Hollingsworth and Matthews neither appear to have any reason for robbery, they both seem to be quite comfortable financially. They are also both family men, on the face of it happily married, I can't really see either them as killers. The man we are looking for is quite cold blooded."

"It could be somebody who uses the newsagents and is aware of Mr Watkins' movements." said the Sergeant. "I don't think it could have been his assistant, he must have been in the shop all afternoon. It's just this minute occurred to me though that the assistant could be in it with somebody else who actually did the job. He could very easily pass on the manager's movements as soon as he left the shop and as those movements had become somewhat of a habit over the past few weeks only very brief instructions would be needed."

"In that case he would be in danger too. The killer would be unlikely to let him live and perhaps tell the tale even if he was the one who set up the robbery. The gunman has already killed at least twice, perhaps four times, this man doesn't hesitate to kill. By the way, do we know yet if there was a telephone or two way radio in the car?"

"The preliminary forensic report is here on your desk guv, there's no mention of anything other than a normal car radio/cassette, cars rarely have telephones these days but he could, of course, have been carrying a mobile 'phone in his pocket. There's no way of knowing that."

"So it's possible that no message at all may have been sent to them that Mr Watkins had boarded the bus. The killer could have either known beforehand that he was on the bus, which could point to somebody from the shop, or assumed that he would be on the bus because he had been every week previously. Of course, it's still possible that the dead driver was in on it. If that was the case then most probably Hollingsworth is implicated otherwise why change shifts? He didn't have to work on his bathroom that day. The trouble with that argument is that Thompson appears to have even less of a reason for robbery than either Hollingsworth or Matthews, also, if he was in on it why try to close the bus doors? It just doesn't make sense. Personally, at this stage, I think that Thompson was probably the innocent victim of a lunatic with a gun, but we must bear all alternatives in mind."

The Sergeant was still reading through the forensic report. "It says here, Guv, that the bullet that killed the youth in the car was definitely fired by the same gun that killed the bus driver."

"Now why doesn't that surprise me?" replied the Inspector, "If only we could find that gun we would have our man. Somehow I don't think he's going to get rid of it. I rather think it probably gives him a feeling of power, it would be like throwing away his right arm."

At that moment a detective constable knocked on the door and entered the room.

"I've been round the hairdressers in town as you asked, Guv" he said, "Julian's Salon in the High Street had Mrs Matthews booked in at two o'clock on Tuesday afternoon. She had a full cut and perm and left at about four thirty. None of the staff there can remember anybody being with her, they were quite positive that she arrived and left on her own."

"So, Geoff Matthews' alibi is now as open and useless as Stan Hollingsworth's." said the Inspector. "It doesn't take a man two and a half hours to buy a pair of trousers, what else was he up to?"

"Every turn we take so far seems to make things more complicated." said the Sergeant. "We seem to be getting further away from a solution every time we see somebody."

"It does rather seem like that at the moment," replied the Inspector. "but don't despair! Sometime soon someone's going to make a mistake. They always do. Come on, it's about time we saw this maintenance engineer, Davies. He should be home by now. Let's see what he has to say for himself."

Chapter eight

As the car driven by Detective Sergeant Tully pulled up outside the bungalow at number 55 Orchard Avenue it was immediately apparent to him, and also to his passenger, that this place was quite different to both the immaculate house of the Hollingsworth's and the cosy abode of the Matthews'.

The bungalow itself was small with two rooms at the front, on either side of the front door and entrance hall, and another room at the back together with the kitchen and bathroom. The once white paint work on the outside of the bungalow was peeling and the front garden, which was surrounded by a picket fence in similar condition, was overgrown with weeds. Down one side of the bungalow a long concrete driveway led to a recently built garage which appeared to be almost as large as the house. Three cars were parked in line down the driveway and a fourth stood on ramps in the garage with its bonnet open.

As the two policemen got out of their car a man, wearing dungarees and a woolly hat and wiping his hands on a rag, came out of the garage and walked down the driveway towards them.

"Mr Davies?" asked Detective Inspector Harty.

"That's me." replied the man, "Having trouble with your car? Or do you want it serviced? Whichever it is I'm your man."

The policemen held out their warrant cards for him to see and the older one said "I'm Detective Inspector Harty of West Town C.I.D. and this is Detective Sergeant Tully. We would like a few moments of your time, Mr Davies, to ask you some questions."

"Oh, I've been expecting you." said Harry Davies, "It's about this bus robbery business, isn't it? Nasty to-do that was I must say. Don't know what the world's coming to. It's about time they brought back hanging. You'd better come indoors we don't want to talk out here."

The policemen followed him up the drive and round to the back of the bungalow where they could not help noticing that the back garden, which was quite large despite the garage, was in total contrast to the front. Colourful spring and early summer flowers abounded and a well-kept lawn sloped gently towards an ornamental pond.

"That's Sylvie's, my wife's, garden," said Harry Davies noticing their surprise. She keeps it nice, doesn't she? The front's a tip I know but I just don't get any time to spare to do anything with it. One thing though, it does keep nosey neighbours away, the women at least. Their husbands bring their cars here for me to see to because I've got a good reputation and don't charge the earth, but their toffee nosed wives won't let them stay to talk which suits me down to the ground."

He led them into the kitchen where Sylvia Davies was wiping up dishes and putting them away.

"Hello love," he said, "We've got the police here about the bus robbery. Put the kettle on, I'm sure they'd like a cup of tea, I know I would." Turning to the policemen he said, "Now, how can I help you?"

"I'm told that you knew the dead bus driver, Peter Thompson, quite well." said Inspector Harty.

"No, I wouldn't say I knew him well." replied Davies, "All right, I spoke to him at work but that's all, I had nothing to do with him otherwise. I felt sorry for the chap. His wife divorced him some years ago and no one else seemed to have any time for him at all, except Stan Hollingsworth, that is. Pete was a real loner, wouldn't join in anything. That sort of thing gets up the lads backs you know, but he couldn't help it, it was just the way he was. I don't really know what Stan saw in him, to tell you the truth, but I think they go back a long way."

"What did you talk to him about?"

"Oh, everything and nothing really, whatever came up at the time. We didn't have a lot in common but I can talk the hind leg off a donkey on any subject given the chance."

"Were you able to find out what his interests were during any of these conversations?"

"I know he was into computers. I don't know much about them myself but he seemed very knowledgeable and was right up to date with the latest developments. He could get quite boring on that subject but he wouldn't talk much about what he actually did on the thing. I tried asking him more than once but, apart from telling me that he used it for word processing and the like, he would say that I wouldn't understand and changed the subject. I only asked him about it to try to make conversation I wasn't really bothered one way or the other."

"What were you doing on Tuesday afternoon between two and four?" asked Inspector Harty.

"Me?" exclaimed Davies, "I was at work. Actually I was out on a job. You probably know that I'm a maintenance engineer. One of the buses had broken down on the route, as usual, and I went out to get it going again. Most of those buses are on their last legs you know, should have been replaced years ago. Still, I shouldn't complain, it keeps me in work."

"Where had the bus broken down?"

"Oh, it was nowhere near the bus that was robbed, if that's what you're getting at. It was over the other side of town, route fifty-one, half way down Conway Street. One of the water hoses had blown, they're a sod to replace. I finished it at about half past three and went straight back to the depot."

"Were you alone while you carried out the repair?"

"No, the driver was there. He mustn't leave his bus while it's out on the road unless it's completely out of service, in which case it's towed back to the garage. One of the rules of the company that is."

"What was the name of the driver?" asked Sergeant Tully.

"Fred Dickens." replied Davies, "He's been on the buses about a year longer than me. A good driver and well liked."

"How long have you been working with the buses Mr Davies?" Inspector Harty asked. "Just over five years, it's a good job and the pay's not bad, I like it. My first love was cars though and still is. Most of my spare time is spent on cars as Sylvie will tell you. I don't know how she stands it sometimes but she's a good lass and she's got her garden. I started out as a fitter in a garage when I was fifteen and have been at it ever since. There was a time when I was in the States, America you know, for about three years. Worked on the railways as a fitter but didn't like it. The money was good though. Then I came back here and met Sylvie, we got married, bought this bungalow and I got the job with the bus company."

"Do you specialise in any particular make of car?" asked the Inspector.

"No. They're all the same to me. Different manufacturers have different ways of doing certain things, especially the foreigners, but basically they're all the same. I manage to keep up to date with developments like fuel injection and cats, catalytic converters to you, and modern cars use a lot of electronics which are out of the scope of most D.I.Y. owners. That's why they like coming to me, I've got all the equipment and do a good job at a fraction of the price a garage would charge. If either of you ever want anything done to your cars you know where to come."

"Thanks, we'll bear that in mind." said Inspector Harty. "Do you ever employ anyone to help you with these cars? Youngsters for instance, there are plenty of them about who are only too keen to mess about with cars."

"Good lord no!" replied Harry Davies, "I prefer to do the job myself, know that it's done properly then. I can't be bothered with keeping an eye on what they might be doing and checking over everything. Besides, they would want to be paid, nobody does anything for nothing these days. Once you start on that lark it leads to all sorts of problems and the tax people start sticking their oar in. No, it's a much easier life if you work alone."

"I expect you get youngsters coming round though." said Sergeant Tully, "A place like this with a garage like yours and all that equipment must be an attraction to them."

"They did at first," said Davies, "but I didn't encourage them. They eventually got the message and they stay away now."

"How do you manage to get hold of the equipment you need?" asked Inspector Harty, "I glanced into your garage as we came past just now and some of it looks pretty expensive. I wouldn't have thought a maintenance engineer's pay would stretch to that sort of thing."

"It doesn't," replied Davies, "but Sylvie and I don't need a lot and all the money I get from doing the cars goes into buying anything that has to be replaced. Most of it was bought when I came back from the States, as I said the money was good and I had a nice little packet to start me off."

"I think that's about all we need to know for now Mr Davies," said Detective Inspector Harty, "but it's possible we may need to speak to you again later to clarify one or two points. You have been very helpful and what you have told us will no doubt enable us to fit one or two more pieces into the jigsaw."

"Only too pleased to help," replied Davies, "the sooner you get hold of whoever killed Pete Thompson the better as far as I'm concerned. It's coming to something when you can't even take a bus ride without worrying about what's likely to happen."

"Oh, I should think this is a one off," said the Inspector, "it's very unlikely to happen again. Thank you for the tea Mrs Davies, I hope we haven't been too much of an interruption."

On the way out the Inspector made a point of having a closer look at the garage and its contents and complimented Davies on its professionalism and completeness.

Sergeant Tully looked over the cars standing on the driveway and asked, "Which of these cars is yours Mr Davies?"

"None of them," replied Davies, "they are all here for servicing. I don't have a car, my van's parked across the road there." He pointed to a white Ford Transit which had seen better days. "That's much more practical for my purposes and Sylvie doesn't mind. We don't go out anywhere very much, shopping mostly."

As the two policemen drove away in their car Sergeant Tully said, "I noticed you didn't mention the second murder, the lad in the car, Guv."

"No," replied the Inspector, "we shall keep that to ourselves for the time being, see how things develop."

"What did you make of Davies, Guv?"

"We seem to have there a prime suspect except that he couldn't have done it if he was on the other side of town at the time repairing a broken down bus. He is always in need of money to satisfy his obvious obsession to keep his garage equipment completely up to date. That could be the motive for the robbery. He has easy access to any car that he wants. He wouldn't use one of his customer's cars if he intended to burn it but he must know how to get hold of a car that would suit his purpose. Despite what he says it would be a very simple matter for him to round up three youngsters who would do almost anything he told them to for the chance to mess around with cars in that garage of his. He knows the bus routes and the workings of the buses, he also knew the driver Thompson who could have recognised him and so signed his own death warrant. He told us himself that he had spent some time in America where guns are all too easy to get hold of. It would be a relatively simple matter to smuggle one, or more, over here."

"He is certainly more likely to be our man than either Hollingsworth or Matthews," said Sergeant Tully, "I shall get things under way to find out as much about him and his movements as possible."

"Good," said the Inspector, "and we must see the driver of that bus he was repairing, Dickens, wasn't it? At the earliest opportunity.

Chapter nine

As Detective Inspector Harty entered the incident room the following morning Detective Sergeant Tully dismissed the constable he had been talking to and walked over to greet him.

"We've had our first bit of luck, Guv," he said, "the dentists in Wirral Road have matched the teeth of our corpse in the car with their records, he was a local lad named Francis Prescott. He had a tooth extracted two years ago when he was sixteen. A couple of fillings a month or so later remove all doubt that he is the right one. His birthday is the twentieth of June, so he would have been nineteen next month."

"Is he known to us?"

"No, Guv, I've checked with the uniform lads too, they've nothing at all under that name."

"What's the address? We'd better make our way round there straight away." said the Inspector.

"35, Blakely Road, it's on the council estate up by the railway."

"So, the poor lad was killed virtually on his own doorstep. I wonder if the killer knew that? The deeper we get into the case the less I like this bloke. The sooner we get him the better I think. Right, come on Bob, let's see what we can find out in Blakely Road. We had better take WPC Wright along with us. If the lad's mother is there this is going to come as a terrible shock to her."

The houses in Blakely Road, and the roads around it, were typical of the council estates that sprang up all over the country in the fifties. Rows of houses, all the same, with small front gardens and side entrances leading to the back. A number of them had been bought from the council by the occupants and attempts had been made to make these more individual thus adding a degree of variety to the overall outlook. The estate as a whole was clean and well maintained.

The front door of number 35 was opened by a woman of about forty. She was rather plump with a pleasant, kindly looking face wearing no make-up. She was dressed in navy blue slacks and a light blue blouse and had slippers on her feet. Her short, brown hair had been roughly brushed without too much care and she was obviously in the middle of her household chores, the vacuum cleaner could be seen where she had left it just inside the living room door.

"Mrs Prescott?", asked the Inspector.

"Yes, that's me," she said, eyeing them suspiciously, "what do you want? It's no good trying to sell me anything, I won't buy anything at the door!"

WPC Wright entered the gate and walked up the path having secured the car and, at the same time, the Inspector showed Mrs Prescott his warrant card.

"I am Detective Inspector Harty of West Town CID," he said, "and this is Detective Sergeant Tully and WPC Wright. Can we come in?"

"Good heavens," she said, a worried look spreading across her face, "what on earth's happened? I've never had the police here before. Has there been an accident? Is it one of the kids?"

"We don't want to talk on the doorstep Mrs Prescott," said the Inspector, "please can we come in?"

"Of course," replied Mrs Prescott. She opened the front door wide and pointed to the living room door. "You'd better go in there, mind you don't trip over the vacuum cleaner I was just starting when you knocked."

The three waited for her to settle herself then the Inspector said, "There's no easy way to say this, Mrs

Prescott, but I'm afraid we have some bad news for you. You have a son named Francis I believe?"

"Frankie?", asked Mrs Prescott now very alarmed, "What's happened? Has there been an accident? Is he all right?"

"You'd better sit down," said the Inspector, beckoning WPC Wright to sit on the settee beside her. "I'm sorry to have to tell you that he has been killed, Mrs Prescott. No, it wasn't an accident, it's worse than that, he's been shot, murdered."

"Frankie dead! Murdered?" exclaimed Mrs Prescott in disbelief, "Who shot him? Why?"

"We don't know yet who did it or why, I wish we did." said the Inspector. "I am very sorry to come out with it so bluntly but there was no other way."

"But Frankie hasn't been in any trouble before." sobbed Mrs Prescott, "He's a good boy, always has been. I just don't understand. It doesn't make sense. What's it all about?"

"Can your husband be contacted?" asked the Inspector, "It would be better if I could talk to you both."

"He left me years ago, I don't know where he is and don't care. I've brought up Frankie and his two sisters on my own for the past ten years or so. Lovely kids, they've all been as good as gold."

"I expect you have read about the bus hold up on Tuesday, or have seen it on television," said Inspector Harty, "We have reason to believe that your son, Frank, was involved and was shot as a direct result of that involvement."

Tears were streaming down the face of Elsie Prescott, a face now distorted with grief and alarm. WPC Jenny Wright did her best to try to comfort her but knew that the worst was yet to come.

"My Frankie wouldn't get mixed up in anything like that, I know he wouldn't!" Elsie Prescott cried, "How do you know it's him? I want to see him."

"I'm afraid there is no doubt that it is your son, Mrs Prescott," said the Inspector, "I don't quite know how to tell you this, I don't want to cause you any more alarm than I need to, but, you see, his body was very badly burned after he was shot and we were only able to identify him from his dental records. What I can tell you is that death was very quick, he wouldn't have suffered."

Elsie sobbed uncontrollably for a few minutes while the two policemen stood quietly by and the policewoman quietly comforted her. Then she pulled herself together, wiped her eyes and face with a handkerchief she drew from the sleeve of her blouse and looked up at Inspector Harty.

"How was he burned?" she asked, "How could it happen? None of this makes any sense, I can't believe it's happening."

"I don't want to go into too much detail at this stage, Mrs Prescott," said the Inspector, "I think it would be too distressing for you. The car he was in caught fire and is burnt out. The pathologist is absolutely certain that your son was dead before that. He was shot in the head at close range, death was instantaneous."

"I must see him," she said, "I must be sure it's him, you do understand, don't you?"

"Yes, I do understand," said the Inspector, "but I must warn you that the body is unrecognisable, it is not something I would recommend. We would normally require a formal identification from a close relative but, in this case, the dental records are sufficient."

"I'm his mother, I shall know. I've got to see him, I shall never be satisfied until I do."

"Very well, Mrs Prescott, Sergeant Tully and WPC Wright will take you to see him. I must ask you some questions about your son but shall do that later if you wish. I can arrange for WPC Wright to stay with you for a while, unless you would rather be left alone."

"It's been a terrible shock and will probably catch up with me later," said Elsie Prescott, "but I would rather answer your questions now. I must know what Frankie has been up to, I thought he was in with a good bunch of lads, what went wrong?"

"That we shall endeavour to find out. Did he live here with you?", asked the Inspector.

"No, he left home in July last year, just after his eighteenth birthday, but he came home to see me and his sisters quite often. He shared a flat with an old schoolmate, Phil Jameson, they had been friends since first starting school. I didn't want him to go but he wanted his independence and I wasn't going to stand in his way."

"Can you give me the address? I must see this Phil Jameson, he could be in danger."

"It's number 149a, Berwick Road, a house that's been converted into two flats. Frankie and Phil had the upstairs one, it's very nice, they were lucky to get it."

"Apart from Phil Jameson did your son have any other close friends?"

"I don't really know, There were a couple of lads he used to see a lot of when he was at school, I can't remember their names, I think one was Craig, but whether or not he was still seeing them I couldn't say. He never mentioned them."

"He hadn't been reported as missing although nobody could have seen him since Tuesday, doesn't that seem strange?" said the Inspector.

"Well, he was here at the weekend. I was beginning to wonder when he was coming round again but he had his own life to lead, I wouldn't have worried unless I didn't see him again this coming weekend. I don't know about his flatmate though, Phil must have wondered where Frankie was unless he was with him, of course."

Realisation of the meaning of her words suddenly hit Elsie Prescott and tears escaped from her eyes again as she said, "I can't believe I shall never see him again."

"I can carry on with these questions later if you wish." said Inspector Harty.

"No, I shall be all right." she replied.

"What did your son do for a living? Did he have a job?"

"He did until last month, he had a lovely job as trainee mechanic at the Willow Garage in Willow Road. Frankie loved working with cars, he's been there since he left school two years ago. Doing very well he was too."

Detective Sergeant Tully said "Willow Garage went out of business last month, Guv, quite suddenly, it surprised everybody when they closed down. It seemed to be quite a prosperous business from the outside."

"I bet that was why my Frankie went off the rails." said Mrs Prescott, "If only he had come to me if he wanted money, but he was so independent, he just wouldn't take anything from me. He told me only last weekend that money wasn't a problem but I know that he didn't have very much."

"It could well be the reason for him becoming involved in the robbery," said the Inspector, "perhaps we'll know more if we find the other two lads in it with him. Did your son ever mention a man named Harry Davies?"

"No, I don't think so, the name doesn't sound familiar." replied Elsie Prescott, "Was he one of the robbers?"

"No, or rather we don't know, it's just a line of enquiry. Mr Davies, like your son, is very interested in cars and car mechanics. I wondered if their paths had crossed at any time."

"Not as far as I know but he didn't tell me everything so it is possible. Frankie was a lovely lad and we are a close family but he found it difficult to talk so I don't know much about who he knew outside."

"Just one more question for now, Mrs Prescott, did Frank have a car?"

"No. I do know he was hoping to get one someday from that garage where he was working. He was a very good driver you know, passed his test first time just after his seventeenth birthday. He's wanted a car of his own for as long as I can remember. He was so happy when he got that job, it must have broken his heart when the garage closed down."

"Well, I'm so sorry to have to give you such bad news, Mrs Prescott, but thank you for answering my questions, it was extremely helpful. Sergeant Tully and WPC Wright will take you to the mortuary now, if you still want to go."

"Yes please, I must go and see him, but I must be back before the two girls come home from school, this is going to be a terrible shock for them, they love their big brother. He would do anything for them."

Tears began to flow again as Elsie Prescott thought of her three children.

To Sergeant Tully Inspector Harty said, "I shall walk round to the lad's flat in Berwick Road, Bob, while you and WPC Wright take Mrs Prescott to see the body. Meet me round at the flat after you have brought her back home."

To Elsie Prescott he said, "We can arrange for WPC Wright to stay with you and your daughters for the rest of the day if you wish. It may be of help to you when you break the news to them. Please let the Sergeant know what you decide."

Number 149 Berwick Road was one of a row of about twenty houses, all of which had been converted into flats and which must provide a healthy income for the owner. Detective Inspector Harty knocked at the front door. Number 149a was the upstairs flat but there was no separate entrance to it, the original hall and stairway being common to both. After a few minutes the door was opened by an elderly man who looked at him rather suspiciously.

The Inspector showed him his warrant card and introduced himself.

"Where's your car?" asked the old man looking up and down the road, "Never seen a copper without a car before, leastways not one in plain clothes."

"I've come to see the young man who lives upstairs." said the Inspector ignoring the man's remark.

"There are two of them, which one do you want?"

"Phil Jameson, he does live here doesn't he?"

"Yes, but neither of them are here at the moment, haven't seen them for most of the week."

"Isn't that unusual?" asked the Inspector.

"None of my business," replied the man, "I keep myself to myself, I don't want to know what they're up to."

"Will you let me in? I would like to take a look round their flat."

"Don't suppose I've much choice."

The Inspector entered the hall and made his way up the stairs, saying as he did so, "My Sergeant will be here soon, please send him up when he arrives."

The man mumbled something unintelligible and went into his own flat.

The upstairs flat consisted of four rooms. The original bathroom remained while the front room, formerly the master bedroom, was now the living room, the box room, next to it, had been converted into a small kitchen and the back bedroom held twin beds, two small wardrobes and two chests of drawers. Considering the flat was normally occupied by two teenaged lads the Inspector was pleasantly surprised to find it remarkably clean and tidy.

His first priority was to find any indication of the whereabouts of Phil Jameson. The man downstairs had said they both hadn't been seen recently so it was reasonable to assume that he had been involved in the bus robbery with Frank Prescott. He realised now that he should have asked Mrs Prescott about Jameson's family and whether Jameson was in work. He made a mental note to ask her later.

He found that a sideboard in the living room had two drawers each of which had been allotted to hold the separate letters and documents for each boy. In Jameson's drawer he found evidence that the lad had been on the dole for some time, further reason to assume he was part of the hold-up gang.

On the sideboard was a framed photograph of two lads arm in arm, one was Frank Prescott, there had been many of him at his mother's house, the other must be Phil Jameson.

Apart from unpaid bills and a few letters from family he found nothing else useful in the living room. A quick glance in the kitchen and bathroom showed nothing there either.

As he entered the bedroom he heard a knock at the front door downstairs and, a few minutes later, Sergeant Tully joined him.

"I wouldn't like that job too often." remarked the Sergeant, referring to his visit to the mortuary with Mrs Prescott, "The poor woman was beside herself when she saw the corpse. I'd be the same if it was my son. Jenny Wright's stayed at home with her and is going to help her with her two girls. She's going to find out if there's a relative who can lend a hand, she's also going to keep her ears open for any useful titbits."

"Good," said the Inspector, "a thing like that shouldn't happen to anyone. It's going to hit her hard over the next few days, she will need all the help she can get. Now, Bob, there's a photo' on the sideboard in the front room here, you'd better take it and see if anyone has seen anything of the lad with Frank Prescott. The bloke downstairs should be able to confirm that it is Phil Jameson in the photo'. Try the local pubs and the job centre, he's been on the dole for some while. I've got a couple of letters to him here, I'll call at the addresses on them to see if they know of his whereabouts. With a bit of luck he might be holed up somewhere but I have a nasty feeling he's probably dead. Can't find anything else of any use, you'd better get the forensic boys to go over this flat with a fine toothcomb."

Chapter ten

As the car sped from the scene of the robbery Phil Jameson, who was one of the rear seat passengers, was wondering what he had got himself into. For that matter why on earth had he involved Frank Prescott?

Phil was a pleasant young lad, eighteen years of age but a bit immature. He was five feet eleven inches tall with a good physique but inclined to be slightly overweight and was topped by an unruly mop of dark, almost black, hair. He had started what had appeared to be a promising job with a butchers in town when he left school at sixteen but, along with many others due to the recession, had lost it after nine months and had been on the dole ever since. His dad had lost patience with him six months previously and had told him to get out and fend for himself. Frankie, who had been a very good friend for as long as he could remember, had insisted that he share the flat and they had lived there together in harmony ever since although Phil had often felt a bit uncomfortable at not being able to put more in the kitty.

He looked at Frankie, who was driving the car, and thought "He doesn't deserve any of this, he's a decent bloke who has done all he can to help me until he lost his job a month ago. Now, because I got him into this, we're both probably involved in murder. None of this was supposed to happen."

"Why did Jimmy have a real gun and why did he have to use it?" he thought to himself as he looked at the man in the front passenger seat. "Why on earth shoot the bus driver? We had done what he wanted and robbed the passengers, it wasn't necessary to shoot the driver, he must be mad."

He then glanced at the lad sitting next to him who returned his look with frightened eyes. He knew very little about the lad, except he was called Tim. Phil had met him for the first time only the previous Thursday evening. It also crossed his mind that he actually knew very little about Jimmy who had roped him into this mess. He had known Jimmy for only a couple of weeks and the way the job had been put to him together with the money offered had been hard to resist. Phil had no idea of the man's full name but Jimmy was what he had told them to call him, he had said it was better that way, the less they knew about each other the harder it would be to incriminate each other if caught. Phil had thought at the time that it was strange for Jimmy to put it like that when only a little earlier he had assured them that the bus hold up was only a stunt but, as gullible as he was, had thought little more about it. He wished now that he had taken more notice of what was said. Everything had seemed logical at the time but now, thinking back, although they knew nothing about him, Jimmy must know who they are and where to find them. He had killed once in cold blood. What was there to stop him killing the three of them to keep them quiet?

The more Phil thought along these lines the more worried he became. Frankie had spotted early on that the guns they had been given weren't real, although they looked genuine enough, and would certainly frighten anybody into giving up their money and valuables.

They had thought, naively, that all four guns must be replicas but now knew better. All the same, it was utter madness to turn a simple robbery, which couldn't have yielded very much cash anyway, into the much more serious crime of murder. Surely it hadn't been necessary. Phil couldn't make out what the man was thinking about when he pulled the trigger. None of it made sense to him.

At this point the car pulled up at traffic lights. Without giving it a second thought Phil pulled at the door handle, flung open the door, jumped out and slammed the door shut behind him. He had never acted so spontaneously in his life before. He ran across the road and, as he did so, heard another car door slam. He felt his muscles tighten as he waited for the gun shot he expected to hear but nothing happened. Continuing to run he couldn't resist looking back and saw that the other lad, Tim, had followed his example and was running round the corner on the other side of the road. Meanwhile the traffic lights had turned green and the car was moving off. So Jimmy was still in the car and so was Frankie.

Phil didn't like deserting Frankie in this way but considered it was the only possible way he could help him. If they were both still in the car then they were both at the mercy of the man. At least, this way, Phil could work out a method of getting to Frankie and, perhaps, help him get away from Jimmy. Of course it was possible that Jimmy had no intention of hurting any of them but, having seen him shoot the bus driver without hesitation, he knew instinctively they were all in danger.

He must try everything he could to help Frankie. Jimmy had said they would make for the old railway sidings after the robbery to dump the car and share the loot, that's where he would head for now. He had no idea what he would do when he got there but, hopefully, some opportunity would arise.

Phil arrived at the sidings and made his way as noiselessly as possible towards the building he knew they were going to use to dump the car. He and Frankie had often played here in their school days so he knew the area well. They had been forbidden to do so by their parents and teachers because of the dangers but that had been part of the attraction. As he got close to the building he heard what sounded like a gun shot. He froze, fearing that he was, after all, too late to do anything to help Frankie. The sound was different to the three shots he had heard in the bus so he hoped he was wrong, but he soon realised that he had heard them in the confined space of the bus and they had therefore been louder.

He managed to stay out of sight behind a pile of old railway sleepers but had a clear view of the car and what was going on. What he saw confirmed his worst fears and sent a chill down his spine.

Inside the car he could see Frankie slumped over the steering wheel but could see nothing of the man who had shot him. Then he spotted him coming out of the building with a petrol can in each hand. From the way he was carrying them they were obviously full. Phil wondered what he was going to do with them, he hadn't long to wait.

Jimmy put one of the cans down on the ground then proceeded to pour the contents of the other one over Frankie's body and the rest of the car interior. Phil felt an instinctive urge to run across and tackle the man but managed to hold himself back, after all there was nothing now he could do to help Frankie although the thought of what was to come filled him with horror. What he was witnessing was worse than a nightmare. Despite himself he felt tears welling up in his eyes but continued watching the awful scene.

Jimmy threw the empty can to one side, picked up the second one and poured that over the outside of the car then, when empty, tossed it across beside the other. He then took off his duffle coat and scarf and threw them on to the rear seat through the open door. He took a box of matches and a piece of notepaper from the pocket of the jacket he had been wearing underneath the duffle coat, screwed up the piece of paper, lit it and tossed it into the car which immediately erupted into a ball of flames. He then made his way towards the road not bothering to look back at his handiwork.

Phil had watched all of this in absolute horror and disbelief. He cast his mind back to the time, only a couple of weeks ago but it seemed much longer, when the man had first approached him. He had seemed to be quite a pleasant bloke, almost like a kindly uncle. He had assured Phil that the bus hold-up had been very carefully thought out and there would be very little danger although, of course, there must be some risk, there always was in something like that. He had told Phil at some length that none of them would be hurt. If anything went wrong, he had said, the police wouldn't be very happy but it was only a stunt anyway. They might get probation for a first offence if they were unlucky, now this! How stupid he had been! Why on earth had he got involved? Of course he knew why, he was desperately short of cash and wanted to repay Frankie for all his kindness. The bloke had sounded so convincing. If only Frankie hadn't lost his job it probably wouldn't have happened at all, but that was why Frankie came in on it too, he was bitter, he had loved that job and thought his future was made, now he was willing to do anything, just didn't care. Now he was dead!

Phil waited behind the sleepers, not daring to look any more at the burning car, until he was sure that the man was well out of the way. He used the time, as well as he could, to think out his own situation. He had decided not to return to the flat which he had shared with Frankie, Jimmy probably knew about it and would look for him there. He would go to his aunt's place on the council estate instead. He was sure she would put him up for a couple of days, she had said as much in a letter he had received recently. He should be safe there, for a little while at least.

He considered, just for a moment, calling the police and telling them what had happened to Frankie, but that would only get him into deeper trouble, if that was possible. In any case there wasn't much he could tell them about Jimmy. No, he decided against it, at least until he had had more time to think through what he should do. His first priority was to get out of there and away from Jimmy.

On his way to his aunt's it occurred to him that he ought to get rid of the duffle coat he was still wearing. He had left the scarf in the car when he jumped out of it at the traffic lights. The police would be looking for anyone wearing a duffle coat after what had happened that afternoon. He would stand out like a sore thumb.

He went into an alleyway between two shops and, for the first time since the robbery, decided to empty the coat pockets to see what the hold-up had yielded. He had been on the upper deck of the bus taking the passengers' money and things and stuffing it into his pockets while the other lad, Tim, had been covering them all with his gun. The first thing he drew out of the pocket was the gun he had used to threaten the passengers with while taking their valuables. He looked at it with disgust, he knew nothing about guns and disliked them intensely. It had been a huge relief to him when Frankie had told him that it wasn't real, he wouldn't have known otherwise, it looked real enough. He put it back into the duffle coat pocket and took out the rest of the contents.

Phil stuffed fifty-five pounds in notes plus some coins into his trousers pocket. A necklace, bracelet and two pairs of earrings he put back into the duffle coat, as he also did with half a dozen or so credit cards. None of those were any good to him and, if he kept them, would incriminate him quicker than anything else if he was stopped. Then he drew out the bag which had been strapped to the waist of that worried looking bloke at the back of the bus. Jimmy had told them particularly to watch out for something like that before they boarded the bus otherwise he would have missed it.

When Phil opened the bag he realised that it must have been the whole object of holding up the bus. Jimmy must have known that the bloke carrying the bag was going to be on the bus. He took out the wad of bank notes and wondered how much was there. He then found a bank paying-in book showing a total of five thousand, eight hundred and forty pounds.

A cold sweat came over him. He was certain in his mind now that Jimmy would be looking for him and coming after the money. He wasn't safe. The sooner he got to his aunt's place the better. He put all the money into his pocket and threw the bag and paying-in book into one of the three dustbins in the alleyway. He then stuffed the duffle coat into the dustbin, left the alley and continued on his way to the council estate.

It suddenly dawned on him that he was now a danger to anyone he came in contact with, Jimmy would stop at nothing. He couldn't involve his aunt, she had been better to him than his own parents. He would have to find somewhere else to hide.

Three days later there was a knock on the front door of number 237 Thorne Road. Audrey Parkin opened the door to find two men standing there.

"Mrs Parkin?" asked the man nearest the door, "I am Detective Inspector Harty of West Town C.I.D. and this is Detective Sergeant Tully." He showed her his warrant card and continued, "I believe that Philip Jameson is your nephew, is that correct?"

Audrey Parkin was a jolly looking woman of fifty-two. She had the appearance of enjoying life to the full including her food. She was not very tall, about five feet four inches, but very stout with an ample bosom. She had lived in the same house on the council estate, with her husband, for thirty-one years and had brought up four children all of whom were now married with families of their own.

"Yes," she said cautiously, "Phil is my nephew, why do you want to know?"

"Can we come inside?" asked the Inspector, "we would like to ask you some questions and would prefer not to do it out here."

She let them in and showed them into the living room asking as she did so, "What's this all about? Phil hasn't got himself into trouble, has he?"

"Is Jameson staying here with you at the moment?" asked the Inspector.

"No, I haven't seen him for some weeks, why do you ask?"

"We found a recent letter from you to him, in his flat, saying that there is always a room here for him if he needed it." said the Inspector. "He hasn't been seen at the flat since Monday so we wondered if he had taken up your offer."

"Yes, I did write that. The poor lad's going through a bad patch, you see, and I had heard that Frankie, who he is living with, had just lost his job so I made the offer just in case he wanted somewhere to go. His dad has more or less washed his hands of him, you know, but I can't see him on the streets, he's not a bad boy. I still don't understand why you're asking these questions. Why have you been through his things at the flat?"

"I'll be honest with you Mrs Parkin," said the Inspector, "but it will probably come as a shock so please sit down if you will."

"We have reason to believe," he continued as Audrey sat down, "that your nephew was involved in the bus hold-up in Birstal Drive last Tuesday. We know for a fact that Frank Prescott was one of the gang and, as Jameson has not been seen since then and he co-habited with Prescott, it is reasonable to assume that he was also one of the four."

"Frankie involved in a robbery!" exclaimed Audrey Parkin, "I don't believe it, he just couldn't be, he is a lovely lad, he wouldn't do a thing like that. The bus driver was killed, wasn't he? No, I can't believe that either Frankie or Phil was there."

"I'm afraid there is no doubt," said the Inspector, "Frank Prescott is dead, shot by the same gun as that used on the bus driver. We have fears for the safety of Jameson, the sooner we find him the better."

"This is a nightmare," said Mrs Parkin, "I knew things weren't going too well for the boys but I had no idea they were so desperate. Poor Elsie Prescott must be beside herself with grief, she thought the world of her son. Phil can be a bit slow sometimes and is easily led but I wouldn't have believed it of Frankie."

"You are sure you haven't seen anything of Jameson?" Sergeant Tully asked Audrey Parkin, "It would be silly to try to hide him, you wouldn't be doing him any favours and it's a serious crime hiding a wanted criminal."

"If he was here I would tell you." she replied, "He's obviously been a silly lad but I don't condone crime. In any case, from what you've told me, it seems his life is probably in danger, he's got into something here that's way over his head. I'm very worried that nobody's seen him, where can he have got to? I suppose you've been to see his parents?"

"Oh yes," said the Inspector, "but, as you say, they seem to have washed their hands of him, didn't seem all that interested. I can't help wondering how they'll feel if he does turn up dead."

"Don't say that," said Audrey Parkin as she saw them out of the house, "doesn't bear thinking about. If I do hear or see anything of him I'll let you know straight away. I must get round to Elsie Prescott's, the poor thing's going to need all the help she can get over the next few days."

"Thank you very much Mrs Parkin," said the Inspector, "I'm sorry to be the bearer of such news but, rest assured, we shall get to the bottom of this before much longer."

"Wish I had your optimism," the Sergeant said to the Inspector as they walked towards their car, "we don't seem to be getting any nearer to a solution."

As they walked into West Town police station they were met by Detective Constable Robson who was carrying a duffle coat in a clear plastic bag.

"The bins were emptied this morning up by the shops near the council estate." he said, "This was in one of them. As it was in a pretty good condition to be in a bin the refuse collector thought he could make use of it. There's no doubt at all that it was used in the robbery. When he looked in the pockets he found this gun, jewellery and credit cards so brought it straight here. "

Robson held out three more plastic bags, one containing a gun, another a couple of necklaces and assorted rings, bracelets and earrings, and the third about half a dozen or so credit cards.

"Well, there's certainly no doubt that it belonged to one of our bunch," said Sergeant Tully, "but I wonder which one, and why leave that lot behind?"

"I think we can safely assume that it was Phil Jameson's," replied the Inspector, "this gun is another replica so it definitely isn't the gang leader's. We know it can't be Frank Prescott's. It's possible it belonged to the third lad but, from where it was found, I wouldn't mind betting it's Jameson's. So he was on his way to his aunt's after all. I wouldn't mind betting he saw what happened to his friend, Frank, and that's why he dumped his coat and that stuff. There's no money, you notice, he must have kept it, unless he'd already handed it over to the leader, but then, why not the jewellery and cards? It's imperative that we find him soon, I can't help wondering why he didn't get to his aunt's and where he is now. I've a dreadful feeling we may be too late but he may have changed his mind and used the cash to travel further afield. Get someone to make some enquiries at the shops where that coat was found, Bob, it's just possible someone saw something. Take that photograph we found in the flat it may help to jog some memories.

Chapter eleven

"Another body's been found, Guv." said Detective Sergeant Tully as Detective Inspector Harty entered the incident room.

"No, it's not Jameson," he continued when he saw the concerned look that passed over the Inspector's face. "This one is known to us. Tim Priestley, seventeen, lived in the fourth floor flats at Bascombe Square. Been in trouble of one sort or another since the age of ten, mostly petty stuff, stealing from shops and cars but, this time, it seems, got in right over the top of his head and paid for it."

"Is he the third one of our young bus robbers?" asked the Inspector.

"Pretty sure he must be but there's no absolute proof yet. Doctor Perry reckons he's been dead about thirty six hours. He was found in a ditch at the edge of the park, not far from the South Gate entrance. Two young boys with a dog found him."

"How was he killed? Shot through the head, I suppose, that seems to be our man's trade mark."

"No," replied the Sergeant, "this one was stabbed, at least three times. I think it was probably too close to the houses to risk using a gun this time, would have been noticed and the alarm would have been raised too soon. There are signs of a violent struggle on the grass by the ditch where the body was found so there's little doubt that he was killed there."

"What makes you so sure he's one of our gang?" asked the Inspector, "Anything else there to point to it?"

"No, just a gut feeling, Guv, he's about the right age, he's the type to get drawn in to something like that and his murder, although with a different weapon, fits in with the characteristics of this case."

"Fair enough," said Inspector Harty, "let's get over to Bascombe Square and see what we can find out. Better take WPC Wright along with us."

The flats in Bascombe Square were of the high rise type that quickly tens to degenerate into a ghetto where petty crime is commonplace and neighbours have as little to do with each other as possible. The door to number 155, Merton House was opened by a tall blonde woman of about twenty-seven. She was dressed in a white blouse and blue denim jeans and had on her feet a pair of dirty trainers. She was holding in her arms a baby girl about eighteen months old and did not seem very pleased at seeing the two men standing there.

"Good morning," said the Inspector holding forward his warrant card, "I am Detective Inspector Harty of West Town C.I.D. and this is Detective Sergeant Tully. I am sorry if we have called at an inopportune time but we must speak to you. May we come in?"

The woman let them both in and closed the door behind them saying, "What's Tim done this time? I suppose it's to do with him? It usually is, must be more serious than normal to involve a detective inspector."

"May I ask what your relationship is with the boy?" said the Inspector, "It would be better if we could speak with his parents."

"I wish you could!" she exclaimed, "He's nothing but trouble. I'm his sister, Tina. Our parents were killed in a car accident when he was eight, he was in the car, in the back, but wasn't hurt. I have looked after him ever since. It's been an enormous strain on my marriage, I can tell you, but my husband's been very understanding, I've been very surprised, at times, at what he's put up with. Now tell me, what's Tim been up to? He didn't come home last night but he's been doing that a lot just lately."

"You had better sit down," said the Inspector, "I'm afraid we have bad news for you. Your brother, Tim, was found dead this morning."

"Tim, dead? I don't understand, how did he die?" she asked, looking at the two policemen with disbelief in her eyes.

"You'd better get WPC Wright in, Bob," said the Inspector, "get her to make a cup of tea." Then returning to the woman, he said, "We have to tell you he was murdered, I'm afraid, stabbed. We have reason to believe he may have been involved in the bus robbery in Birstal Drive last Tuesday and was killed because of that."

"I knew he'd get into serious trouble one day," Tina said, "but never dreamed it would be anything like this. Why was he killed? He didn't deserve to die, he was still so young!"

"We don't know yet why he was killed," said the Inspector, "but it seems that the man who organised the bus robbery and killed the bus driver doesn't want anybody left who can identify him, or else he's just plain mad and killing for the sake of it. What can you tell me about your brother?"

"Well, as I said, he's been in trouble before, stealing mostly. He used to be a nice, quiet little boy but he changed after mum and dad died, I think he resented having to answer to me. I was just coming up to eighteen then and he has never really accepted me as being an adult. There was nobody else to look after him, we have no other close relations, but I didn't want him fostered out as he was the only family I had. I married when I was twenty two and my husband agreed to keeping him with us. Rick, my husband, has been marvellous and has put up with a lot from Tim. He will be very upset when he hears about Tim's murder. Deep down, you know, Tim was quite a sensitive boy but had this rebellious streak and refused to respond to discipline. He was a coward too, that's mainly why I'm so surprised he was involved in that bus robbery, I wouldn't have thought he'd have the guts. Stealing from shops and cars is more in his line."

"Very often it's hard for them to refuse to do a job, especially if others are in it too," said Sergeant Tully, "Cowards are usually their own worst enemy and lead themselves into all sorts of scrapes. Has he said anything at all that might give us some pointers?"

"He never told us anything." replied the woman, "I remember he was looking worried when he came home on Tuesday afternoon but we couldn't get anything from him. He went straight to his room and stayed there for the rest of the day, wouldn't even come out for something to eat."

"He came back here then." said Inspector Harty, "We would like to look over his room, if you have no objection."

Tina took them along the corridor and showed them into the room at the back of the flat. It was a typical teenage boy's room decorated in dark colours and with the walls festooned with posters. A single bed stood in the corner with the duvet left as it had fallen when the occupant had climbed out. Clothes were strewn untidily about the floor and on the only chair in the room and a pile of records and cassettes formed a small cascade beside a chest of drawers on top of which was a cheap stereo hi-fi system. A small wardrobe and a table holding a portable television set completed the scene.

"This is his room," she said, "he had his meals with us, of course, but most of the time he was home he spent in this room watching telly on that portable or playing records. I'm sorry about the mess but he wouldn't let me touch anything in here"

While she spoke Sergeant Tully had opened the door of the wardrobe and he took out a duffle coat which was hanging there. In one of the pockets he found a black scarf and a gun.

"Look at this, Guv," he said, "leaves us in no doubt now that he was one of the bus robbers."

"Where on earth did he get that gun?" asked the woman, "I didn't know he had that, I wouldn't have allowed it in the place if I'd known. My husband would have had a fit."

"Don't worry," said Inspector Harty, taking the gun from the Sergeant, "it's not real, it's quite a good quality replica that can be bought quite easily. People have them hanging on their walls as showpieces. Apparently, the man who organised the robbery kitted them all out with one of these, the one he had himself, though, was real enough. Do you know where your brother got the duffle coat?"

"No, he came home wearing it on Tuesday, I hadn't seen it before that, but, I must admit, it didn't register too well with me, I didn't take a lot of notice of it. I was more concerned at the worried look on his face, and he was red and sweaty, as if he'd been running. He just went straight to his room and ignored all my questions."

"Has he mentioned anybody else recently?" asked the Inspector. "Somebody, perhaps, new to you?"

"At tea time on Monday he did say he was going to see a couple of blokes but he didn't mention any names, I was a bit annoyed because I wanted him to look after little Susie for me but he just went out anyway. My husband, Rick, said he saw him with two other lads and a man in the bar at the Dog and Hounds round the corner later that evening but didn't talk to him. I don't think Tim even noticed Rick was there."

The Inspector looked up sharply at this last remark. "They were probably meeting to discuss the robbery," he said, "did your husband recognise the man?"

"I don't think so," she said, "I seem to remember Rick saying that his back was towards him but he could tell you when he gets home."

"What time would that be?" asked the Inspector, "This might be the breakthrough we're looking for. Can we get hold of your husband at work?"

"He travels about a lot, I don't know where he'll be during the day. His firm are too mean to give its employees mobile telephones. He usually gets home at around six thirty, you can see him then."

"We'll be here at about eight, if that's all right," said Inspector Harty, "That will give him time to have his tea and get over the shock of hearing about your brother."

"That will be fine," said the woman, "I'll tell him to expect you. He put up with a lot from Tim but that was mainly for my sake. He didn't have a lot of time for him but it'll be a nasty shock all the same."

"Thank you for your help." said the Inspector, "Will you be all right or would you like WPC Wright to stay with you for a while?"

"No, I shall be OK, I'm glad mum and dad aren't here though, Tim was the apple of their eye, they couldn't have taken this."

As they left the flat Inspector Harty said to the Sergeant, "Perhaps we're getting somewhere at last, it will be very interesting to hear what her husband has to say. The pieces to the jigsaw are gradually falling into place at last. From what we know now it is clear that the villain of the piece, the killer, held up the lower deck of the bus while Frank Prescott robbed the passengers there and, on the upper deck, Tim Priestley had the job as hold-up man while Phil Jameson relieved those passengers of their valuables."

"How can you be so sure of that last bit?" asked Sergeant Tully.

"Think about it, Bob, Priestley's duffle coat had only the scarf and gun in the pockets, Jameson's had jewellery and credit cards as well. My first thought had been that Priestly was probably killed at a meeting with the killer for a share out of the loot but, now, I don't think so. Jameson's coat had all the jewellery and cards from the passengers on the upper deck in the pockets but no cash, and the coat had been thrown away, dumped in a dustbin. I don't believe the killer would have got rid of it in that way, Jameson did. I think the killer intended to get rid of all three lads immediately after the robbery but, somehow, Jameson and Priestley got away. The killer has since been looking for them, he's found Priestley, the big question is, has he found Jameson?"

At eight o'clock that evening Detective Inspector Harty and Detective Sergeant Tully were back at Bascombe Square to interview Tim Priestley's sister's husband Rick.

"This is a terrible business Inspector," said Rick, "it's been an awful shock for my wife, I can tell you. Many's the time she has wished Tim wasn't living with us, especially since Susie was born, but neither of us wanted it this way. She's done everything possible to make life easy for him but he's never given her any thanks for it."

"I can understand how you feel, sir," said the Inspector, "but I am hoping you can give me some information that may lead me to the killer. I understand from your wife that you saw Priestley at the Dog and

Hounds on Monday evening with three other people, is that right?"

"Yes, Inspector, he didn't see me, he was too engrossed in what they were saying, and I didn't like him enough, I must admit, to let him know I was there. I was going to speak to him later about being in that bar, he shouldn't have been there, he's under age. Anyway, I only saw them briefly as I left the bar to come home. They were sitting at one of the little round tables. Two of them were about the same age as Tim, perhaps a little older, but the other one, I would say, was probably about fortyish. It crossed my mind, knowing Tim as I do, that they were probably up to no good."

"Can you describe the older man?"

"He had his back to me, unfortunately, so I didn't see his face, he was wearing a hat, a trilby that's seen better days, and a duffle coat or donkey jacket, not sure which. He had quite a broad back and looked as if he might have been fairly tall, although it's difficult to tell when they're sitting down. I've been caught out like that before."

"Do you know if you'd seen him before?"

"I don't think so, no, I'm sure I haven't. I don't go to the pub very often and don't really notice people when I do. I was there that night because I'd been driving around a lot and fancied half a lager before I went home. It was only because of Tim, and the fact he shouldn't have been there, that I noticed what I did."

"I don't suppose you heard anything that was said?" asked the Inspector.

"I was too far away to hear anything and bars are quite noisy anyway, that one was no exception, sorry!"

"Well, thank you for the information, sir," said Inspector Harty, "I don't think there's anything else at the moment. If you should happen to think of anything please let us know at the station."

"That description could fit either Stan Hollingsworth, Geoff Matthews or Harry Davies." said Sergeant Tully when they had left the flat.

"And thousands of others!" retorted the Inspector, "We've got to keep an open mind, Bob, there's no evidence at all, so far, to link Hollingsworth, Matthews or Davies to the crime. The Dog and Hounds isn't the local for any of them, by any chance?"

"No, Guv, it's quite a distance, though not too far, from all of them. I should hardly think they'd use their local for a meeting like that anyway, would be madness if they did. I'll get someone to check out the Dog and Hounds, perhaps the staff there might remember something. It's also possible that the regulars may be able to help. They often notice if strangers are around, especially if they might be acting suspiciously."

"Right, Bob, we'll get together tomorrow and compare notes. Do you know if Robson's got any further with that computer of Thompson's yet? He was having problems with passwords last I heard."

"I don't know, Guv, he hasn't said anything to me, I'll check with him in the morning."

"OK, Bob, let's call it a day, my wife's very understanding but I don't want to take liberties. You'll have to get married, you know, do you the power of good."

"No, I'm all right as I am thanks, Guv, I like my freedom, I'd hate to be tied down. Besides I haven't met anyone yet I'd like to call Mrs Tully. Maybe I'll think about it one day, not just yet though."

Chapter twelve

"Good morning, Bob," said Detective Inspector Harty as he entered the incident room the following morning, "any more developments?"

It was now Saturday, the fourth day after the bus shooting, and the Inspector felt that something more positive about the killer should have come to light by now.

"Not a lot, Guv," replied Detective Sergeant Tully, "but I went round to the Dog and Hounds after leaving you last night to see if I could pick up anything there. Being a Friday night too it was likely that most of the regulars would be there."

"Good man, that's what I call dedication," said the Inspector, "kill two birds with one stone. What's the beer like round there?"

"The beer's O.K. but I don't think much of the place, really gone to the dogs, if you'll excuse the pun, the landlord's a slob and doesn't seem to care what goes on there, or who he serves."

"Not much help then, I gather? To be quite honest I wasn't too hopeful of anything coming out of that pub, I know of its reputation you see, but I suppose it was just possible that someone might be able to identify our man."

"Well, I spoke to the staff and to the regulars and you are right, none of them were very helpful. A couple of them did say they saw the four sitting at a table and one said he heard a name mentioned, sounded like Jimmy, remembered it because it is also his brother's name, but otherwise didn't take a lot of notice. They get a lot of passing trade in that pub and, as far as they are concerned, it's just a matter of giving a drink and taking money from a lot of faces, they couldn't even say whether they were young or not. Nobody remembers seeing them there on any other day apart from Monday so it seems probable that it was just a one off meeting there."

"Jimmy, eh? Well that's something." remarked the Inspector, "At least we can put a name of sorts to our killer. It's the sort of name that a casual acquaintance might give to someone he doesn't know but it's the only lead we've had so far. We now know who the three youngsters were, and none of them could answer to the name Jimmy, so this one could be our man. Could the bar staff say which of them bought the drinks?"

"No, it appears that all four were in a group at the bar talking together when they first went in then, when they were served, they took their drinks and sat at the table. From what I could gather I think they were there for about three quarters of an hour. A thought has crossed my mind though, Guv, for what it's worth. The name, Jimmy, doesn't fit squarely with any of our three main suspects. Perhaps there is someone else in the frame who we haven't even considered yet, either that or one of them is using it to cover himself. Another complication we could do without."

"It's certainly a thought worth bearing in mind, Bob," said the Inspector, "after all we have nothing concrete yet to pin on anybody. It's all very circumstantial against Hollingsworth, Matthews and Davies and we may very well be barking up the wrong tree. You know, though, that men like our killer usually have egos the size of ostrich eggs so you could check on anybody else at the bus garage or the newsagents with the name Jimmy, Jim or James. We'll have to see if we can find out if our four got together in any of the other pubs in the area. They must have had more than that one meeting to sort out the details of the hold up. It would be a big help if we could find out how they first met. It's obvious that the older man must have been the instigator of the robbery but how did he rope in the other three? Did he know them or were they chance acquaintances? I should think the latter, it would take an extremely hard hearted man to kill off youngsters he knew in the way that he has."

"I don't know, Guv," said the Sergeant, "I think the man must be a maniac, I still can't see a real reason for any of the killings, it all seems so unnecessary."

"Oh, I think there's a reason all right, although goodness knows what it is." replied Inspector Harty, "I only wish we could find Jameson. If he did get away from the others after the robbery, and I'm sure he must have done otherwise why dump his coat in that dustbin, then he must still have the bulk of the money with him. After all he was the one on the upper deck of the bus who took the money bag from Watkins, the newsagent manager. I should imagine that is reason enough for our man Jimmy to want to bump him off. I'm assuming for the moment that Jameson is still alive of course. If he isn't we are going to have an uphill struggle proving anything."

"That's another thing I was going to tell you about, Guv, a witness has come forward to say he saw two lads jump out of the rear of a car on Tuesday afternoon, while it was stationary at the traffic lights in Taymor Street. He was driving a car in the opposite direction and was waiting at the lights on the other side of the road junction when the offside rear door of the other car flew open and a lad jumped out and ran across the road like a bat out of hell. Almost immediately the nearside door opened and another lad ran off in the opposite direction. He said he didn't think too much of it at the time, although it seemed a strange thing to do, thought it was just lads mucking about, but thinking about it since, he's sure that it happened at about the time the robbery took place."

"Did he see the driver and front seat passenger? Did they try to stop the other two?"

"No, he was more interested in the two who ran off although he doesn't remember anybody else getting out of the car. The lights changed to green soon after they had jumped out of the car but, by the time he'd moved off they had disappeared down the side streets. He said that he did notice that the two in the front of the car looked back when they jumped out but didn't do anything else. They moved away from the lights at the same time he did."

"The Taymor Street lights are only a few minutes away from where the bus was held up," said the Inspector, "and it's in the right direction for the railway sidings, it has to be the bus robbers. There was hardly time to empty pockets and hand over cash, all the more reason to believe that Jameson still has that money. I wonder if it was a spur of the moment thing for them to run off like that? I should think it must have been because I would hardly think that Jimmy would trust any of the three lads enough to let them go before he had made sure of the loot. Jameson must be holed up somewhere, but where? I was sure he would be at his aunt's. If he was headed there I wonder what made him change his mind?"

"If he's got six thousand quid on him he could be anywhere," replied the Sergeant, "If I was him I'd get as far away as possible, especially if our killer is a local bloke, as it seems he must be."

"Don't forget that Jameson isn't the brightest of lads, at least according to his aunt. No, I think he's still in the area somewhere, probably completely lost for ideas without his friend Prescott to help him. He must be getting pretty desperate. He'll come to the surface soon."

"Changing the subject," continued the Inspector, "have we found anything worthwhile in the bus driver's house, or in Prescott's flat or Priestley's room?"

"D.C. Robson's outside," said the Sergeant, "I'll get him in and see how it's going."

"We've finished searching Thompson's house," said Robson, "found quite a collection of hard porn videos in the bottom of a cupboard."

"Well, it's not a crime to have them in your own home." replied the Inspector, "A lot of men who live on their own resort to those things. For some it's the only way they can get any satisfaction especially if, as it seems with Thompson, they don't get on with women. I don't think it can have any bearing on our case. What's more important have you managed to get into that computer system yet?"

"We've managed to get past one password, Guv, quite a job it was. Usually people with home computers don't bother with passwords or, if they do, use something simple like their own name or an anagram of it. This bloke really didn't want anybody else getting in to his system. Anyway, we've got into a web site which seems to be used for file sharing but have come up against another password which prevents further access so don't yet know what he uses it for."

"That's all double dutch to me," exclaimed the Inspector, "tell me what you mean in plain English."

"His computer runs wireless broadband to get on to the internet," replied Robson, "which uses the telephone system to transmit information between websites. This enables all sorts of files, including pictures, to be transferred from one computer to another very quickly and efficiently. He can then save these files to his own computer's hard drive and so use them however he wishes. There is plenty of software readily available to do it all. This interchange between computer users is very popular and is now a world-wide thing. Much of it, incidentally, is illegal."

"What sort of information would be transmitted?"

"Anything really, most people use it to pass news or tips or even computer programs to each other. With the more sophisticated graphics hardware available these days pictures and videos are very popular things to transmit. With what we know of Thompson's liking for porn I strongly suspect that pornography is what he was sending, and receiving, down the line."

"Computer porn!" exclaimed the Inspector, "I've read about it but, from what I've seen of computer pictures I can't see anybody getting too excited about that."

"Ah, but you haven't seen the latest graphics," replied Robson, "with a high definition LCD screen like Thompson's they're every bit as good as photographs or films on DVD. You don't have to use your imagination it's almost like being there. It's very popular, and there's no age limit. Anybody using the internet has access to them if they are that way inclined."

"The mind boggles," said the Inspector, "modern technology has a lot to answer for. I still can't see that it has anything to do with our case though. If Thompson had to get his kicks that way I feel rather sorry for him. Anything else?"

"Nothing else worthwhile in Thompson's house," said DC Robson, "he seems to have been a lonely sort of bloke all right, certainly nothing there to give any reason why he should have been killed. As soon as we've got past that other password on the computer I'll let you know what we've found."

"Thanks. Now, Bob, what about Prescott's flat? Any clues there?"

"Nothing to link either Prescott or Jameson to anybody else who could have been involved in the robbery." said Sergeant Tully, "Jameson has certainly made no attempt to return to the flat. Apart from bills, most of which seem to have been paid, the only correspondence we've found is from female relatives, Prescott's mother, Jameson's aunt and sister, and that doesn't seem to have been very frequent."

"Well we know that Prescott saw his family quite often," said the Inspector, "no real reason to write, and Jameson didn't get on too well with his parents. No notes or scraps of paper about, I suppose, hinting at a recent meeting anywhere?"

"None that we found, if they did make notes they either kept them on their person or destroyed them. We did find this in Priestley's room though."

Detective Sergeant Tully took a small sheet of ruled paper from his pocket, it had obviously been torn from a pocket note book with a ring binder. On it was written, in pencil, 'Friday, Job Centre, J'.

Inspector Harty read it and said, "The way it's written here it looks as though it was jotted down from a telephone message. Could be anything, of course, but, then again, it could be to do with a meeting last Friday, possibly the first meeting, at a job centre, to set up the robbery. The 'J' could be short for Jimmy."

"That's what I thought, Guv, so I called in at the local job centres to see if anybody had seen anything. Priestley used the one in the High Street and, according to the staff there, so did Jameson. They didn't have Prescott on their books though and nobody could say if Priestley and Jameson knew each other or whether they had met an older man there. They are usually too busy to pay much attention to what others are doing."

"I wouldn't mind betting that Jimmy, or whatever his name is, recruited his gang from the job centre." replied the Inspector, "It makes sense, young lads at a loose end, probably been looking for jobs for weeks and getting a bit desperate. It wouldn't take much to persuade a couple of them to go off the rails. Convince them there's hardly any risk and promise money for old rope."

"The way I see it," he continued, "is, that because Priestley got a telephone call he was probably already known to Jimmy who told him to rope in a couple of other lads from the job centre and meet him there on Friday. Prescott wouldn't have been on the job centre books because he hadn't been out of work long enough to qualify, but Jameson knew what sort of mental state he was in and probably mentioned him as a possible recruit. That would have made it very easy for Priestley who wouldn't now have to look for anyone else. Whether they met Jimmy inside or outside the job centre we don't know but it really doesn't matter. Get a few enquiries going there, Bob, to see if anybody else was approached at all and, if so, how they were asked if they wanted to do the job. Ask around, as well, to see if anybody saw the meeting between Jimmy and the other three. Any information at all, however trivial, could be vital to the case. Is there anything more?"

"I don't know if you've seen Dr Perry's report on the post mortem of Tim Priestley yet, Guv, but there's something there that's unusual and needs thinking about."

"No, I haven't seen it yet. What's the problem?"

"As you know, Priestley was stabbed several times, not shot like the others, but he wasn't stabbed with a knife. Dr Perry says the wounds are more consistent with something like a long screwdriver. There were two wounds in the back and another in the chest, the one in the chest being fatal."

"That's very interesting, Bob, the killer must have had the screwdriver ready to hand. Possibly came across Priestley by accident at the park. What time of the day was he killed?"

"Round about four thirty in the afternoon."

"Yes, that fits," said Inspector Harty, "the killer couldn't possibly use the gun in that area at that time of day without bringing immediate attention to himself. I don't suppose he carries the gun around with him during the day anyway. He could be a maintenance man of some sort, working over by the park somewhere, when he spotted Priestley. Another black mark against Davies perhaps except that, from what we have been told, he couldn't have been involved in the robbery. Then there's Matthews, of course, as a gas fitter he would have ready access to a screwdriver. There couldn't have been anybody else around at the time otherwise the opportunity to kill wouldn't have arisen. He grabbed the screwdriver from his toolbox, or else he was already using it and had it in his hand, came up behind Priestley and stabbed him in the back. The first strike would have taken Priestley by surprise and, before he recovered, he was stabbed in the back again. He fell to the ground where the killer turned him over and, to make absolutely sure, stabbed him a third time, in the chest. He then pushed him into the ditch where, he probably hoped, the body might stay undiscovered for some time. He's already proved that he's a cold hearted sod. I do believe there's a bus route along that side of the park, isn't there Bob?"

"Yes, Guv, I think the buses come from the same depot as the one robbed on Tuesday. That was route thirty-seven, the one past the park is route thirty-nine."

"So, our killer could still be a bus worker, but, like Davies, a maintenance man rather than another driver. Come on, Bob, let's get round to the depot and see if a bus needed maintenance while on its route past the park. We must also have a word with the driver of that bus that Davies was working on Tuesday afternoon, Dickens I think his name was."

"Hello Inspector, Sergeant," The bus depot manager greeted them as they entered his office, "any news for us yet?"

"No," replied the Inspector, "but we have a lead we want to follow up. Did one of your buses break down near the South Gate entrance to the park on Thursday afternoon?"

"Let me see," said the manager, picking up a log book from the corner of his desk, "that'll be route thirty-nine, all breakdowns on the road are logged in this. No, there were no events at all on that route all day Thursday."

"Would there be any other reason for a maintenance man to attend that route?"

"Not that I can think of. Why are you asking?"

"We have very good reason to believe that somebody, probably with a toolbox, was in that area on Thursday afternoon. At this time I can't tell you more than that."

"I'll ask the maintenance foreman." said the manager, picking up the telephone, "Hello, John, you were here last Thursday afternoon, weren't you? I thought so. Tell me, did you have to send anyone out to route thirty-nine that afternoon? Yes, I know it should be in the log book, I just want confirmation. Right, the whole crew were in the workshop all afternoon, you're absolutely sure? John, I just want a definite yes or no, Thanks."

Turning to the Inspector he said, "I expect you got the gist of that. He's adamant that none of his crew left the workshop on Thursday afternoon. I've no reason to think otherwise, he's a bit bolshie but he runs a very tight ship and gets the best from his men. He'd know, and say, if any of them weren't where they were supposed to be."

"Do you have anyone named Jimmy working here?" asked the Inspector, "Not only in maintenance, anywhere in the depot, might be a nickname."

"Jimmy?" queried the manager, "No, nobody of that name here for a while. Bit surprising really, it's quite a common name, usually one or two around."

"OK," said the Inspector, "just a thought. I believe you do have a driver by the name of Dickens. Can you tell me how I can get hold of him?"

"Fred? Yes. He's one of our best men, been here a few years now, straight as a die. Surely you don't suspect him? He's one of the nicest blokes you could wish to meet, I don't think there's an ounce of antagonism in him."

"No, it's nothing like that." replied the Inspector, "We are hoping that he can confirm an alibi we have been given. Perhaps he can clear one of our suspects once and for all."

The depot manager glanced at the clock on the wall of his office and said, "As it happens he should be here now, it's his rest period between runs, he's due out again in about seven minutes. You should be able to find him in the canteen."

"Right, thanks, we shall pop in there and see him, it won't take long." said Inspector Harty, "We won't take up any more of your time. If anything at all comes to mind you will let us know, won't you?"

"Of course." replied the manager as they took their leave.

There were only a handful of men in the canteen and it didn't take long for the two policemen to pinpoint Fred Dickens and introduce themselves to him.

"We would like to ask you a couple of questions, Mr Dickens." said Inspector Harty, "It concerns the robbery on Tuesday afternoon which resulted in the death of your colleague, Mr Thompson."

"I don't quite see how I can be of any help," replied Fred Dickens, "but I shall certainly answer your questions if I can."

"I understand that your bus broke down while you were on your route on Tuesday. Is that right?"

"Yes, it's happening all too frequently these days. You can't begin to understand how inconvenient it can be, not only for the passengers but for us too, but what has that got to do with the robbery?"

"Can you remember at what time it happened?"

"At twenty minutes to two, we have to log all stoppages very thoroughly."

"You had to call out the maintenance engineer. At what time did he arrive and who was it?"

"It was Harry Davies, he arrived at five minutes to two. I was glad it was him, he can always be relied on to get the bus moving again whatever is wrong with it."

"How long did it take him to get it repaired?" asked the Inspector.

"Rather longer than I had hoped," said Fred Dickens, "it was nearly three thirty before he had finished, they really must replace those old buses soon."

"Was Mr Davies working on the bus for the whole of that time?"

"No, he had to go back to the depot for a part he hadn't got in his van. That was the main reason for the job taking so long."

The Inspector looked sideways at Sergeant Tully "Can you tell me how long he was away getting the part?" he asked Fred Dickens.

"Well," Dickens replied, "he had been working on the engine for about ten minutes when he had to go off for the part. He arrived back to finish the job just after three so he was away for just under an hour. When I asked him why it had taken him so long he told me they hadn't got the part at the depot either so he had to go to central stores for it. That's on the industrial estate on the other side of town, a twenty mile round trip from where I had broken down, so it seemed reasonable enough although I wasn't very happy at hanging around all that time."

"How did Davies seem to you when he returned?" asked the Inspector.

"I'm not quite sure what you mean." replied Dickens, "but he seemed all right. I think he was a little bit angry at having to go all that way for quite a small part but he didn't say much, just got on with the job."

"Well thank you very much Mr Dickens," said Inspector Harty, "I won't take up any more of your break period, you have been very helpful. I would be grateful if you would keep our conversation to yourself for the time being."

"That's no problem," replied Dickens, "as far as I'm concerned it's nobody else's business. I'm only too pleased to help."

As Detective Inspector Harty and Detective Sergeant Tully left the canteen to pick up their car the Inspector said, "So all three of our main suspects have no real alibi for the time of the robbery, that's very interesting. I wonder why Davies failed to tell us about going to get the part. I must say though that of the three the cards seem to be stacking very high against Harry Davies. So far everything seems to be pointing towards him being our man."

"Yes, but there was no bus breakdown near the park where Priestley was killed," said Sergeant Tully, "so there was no reason for Davies to be there."

"I know we were told that all the maintenance crew were in the depot that afternoon but he could have been on a private job repairing a car, Bob, and being covered by his mates" replied the Inspector, "don't forget that. But also don't forget that Matthews is a gas fitter and could also have been working in the area so nothing is cut and dried. We'll have to do some more checking."

"It seems a bit too convenient to me for that bus to breakdown when it did on Tuesday afternoon." said the Sergeant, "If Davies is our man it must have been a heaven sent opportunity for him to get out of the depot. Do you think that the driver, Fred Dickens could be in it with him?"

"From what the depot manager said of Dickens and from snippets I've heard elsewhere I shouldn't think so." the Inspector said, "He seems to be a man beyond reproach. No, it's more likely that Davies, with his knowledge of engines, rigged the bus before it went out, purposely selecting one on a route going in an opposite direction to the robbery target. That would give him the perfect excuse for being away from the depot and an alibi for his whereabouts that afternoon all rolled into one. It's a pity for him that he chose a bus with an honest driver.

"Shall I bring Davies in for questioning, Guv?" asked Sergeant Tully.

"No, Bob, not until we've found Jameson. I don't want to alarm anybody unduly at this stage or put anyone on their guard. Besides everything is still very circumstantial at the moment, there is still not a scrap of evidence that either Davies, Matthews or Hollingsworth were involved in the robbery or were anywhere near the bus at the time. The case is still wide open. Anybody could have done it."

Chapter thirteen

At number 16 Berwick Road Freda Hollingsworth was busy in her kitchen preparing the vegetables for the mid-day meal. Her husband, Stan, was sitting at the opposite end of the kitchen table enjoying a cup of coffee and reading the morning newspaper. It was one of his days between shifts at the bus depot and, so far, his intentions for the day had been thwarted by the weather. He glanced out of the window at the rain, which had been falling steadily since he had awoken, and thought of the work he could have been doing in the garden. The bathroom was now complete and, although he was very pleased with the end result, the job had taken much longer than he had expected and the garden had been largely neglected meanwhile although Pete Thompson had spent some time on it before his untimely death.

"Just look at that weather," he said with feeling, "it looks set for the rest of the day. As if we hadn't had enough rain already. It's going to be a quagmire out there by the time I can do anything. I wanted to get those geraniums in the greenhouse planted out before it's too late. If I don't do it today it's going to be another week before I can get around to it."

"Never mind," his wife replied, "the garden really doesn't look too bad and it was very worthwhile spending the time on the bathroom. I showed it off to Jenny yesterday, she was green with envy, her Tom's useless when it comes to D.I.Y."

"He's useless at anything, don't know what Jenny ever saw in him." said Stan, "Tell you what, I'm missing poor old Pete already, it's not the same without him, I don't seem to be able to get in the mood for anything. I know he could be a bit of a nuisance at times but he was handy to have around. His funeral's in a couple of days time, by the way, I'd better get a black tie from somewhere."

"I think Tom might be able to help you there, his mother was buried a couple of months ago, he must have one. I'll ask Jenny next time I see her."

"Don't leave it too long then, I'll have to buy one if he hasn't got one and there isn't a lot of time to go into town before the funeral."

"Oh, don't worry, the supermarket down the road sells ties. They're sure to have a black one. If Jenny can't help I'll pop down there and get one for you. I was wondering, who pays for Pete's funeral? He didn't have any relatives apart from Geoff, did he? I don't suppose a cousin would make a provision for something like that."

"The bus company's dealing with it, after all he was killed while on duty so it's the least they can do. All I hope is that the weather improves before then, it's bad enough at a funeral without having to stand out in the rain as well."

"It always rains at funerals in the films on telly," said Freda, "I suppose it helps to make them more solemn. Have you seen or heard anything more of how the police are getting on? Have they got any idea who did it yet?"

"They've been to the depot a couple of times but haven't spoken to me any more. From what I hear they don't seem to be much further forward. I don't suppose any of us have seen the last of them yet by a long way. Did you know that those two young lads they found dead were part of the gang that robbed Pete's bus?"

"What two young lads?" asked Freda

"The one found burnt to a cinder in a car at the old railway sidings and the other one stabbed, found in a ditch in the park, it was in the papers. You must have seen it"

"I don't remember reading anything about them being connected with the robbery, that's awful."

"Yes, I heard it being talked about at the depot. Apparently there's evidence linking them to the robbery. Didn't do them any good, did it?"

"But they weren't much more than kids, were they! Do you mean to say that a gang of kids robbed the bus and killed Pete!"

"No, I didn't say that. The leader of the gang, the one who shot Pete, was about our age, the other three were youngsters. Now two of them are dead. I don't know for sure but it seems the leader is bumping them off as well. Probably wants all the loot for himself."

"That's terrible!" exclaimed Freda, "he must be a maniac. I hope the police catch him soon. What about the third boy?"

"I don't know," replied Stan, "probably hiding out somewhere, or else he's dead and hasn't been found yet. I really don't know what the world's coming to."

Hollingsworth folded his newspaper and drank the rest of his coffee then, looking out of the window said, "Well, I'm not going to get anything done out there today, that's for sure, might as well watch that video I hired."

"Don't go yet, Stan," said Freda, "I want to talk to you about Claire."

Stan sat down again and said, "What about Claire?"

"Well, I wasn't going to say anything yet but I can't keep it to myself any longer, I'm worried about her."

"Why, what's the matter? What has she done? She seems all right to me. She was her usual self when she went off to school this morning."

"I think she puts on an act for your benefit but I've noticed she's gone off her food lately, especially breakfast, she hasn't had any breakfast for over two weeks now and, this morning, I heard her in the bathroom being sick."

"Probably got a tummy bug, there's a lot of it around. Better get her to go to the Doctor's this evening."

"No, I don't think it's a bug, Stan, judging by the symptoms I rather think she might be pregnant."

"Don't be silly she's only fourteen, she can't possibly be pregnant, I think you're letting your imagination run away with you, Freda."

"I don't think so, Stan. I might be mistaken, hope to God I am, but everything points to it. She may be only fourteen but don't forget she's a young woman now. You still treat her like your little girl but she's growing up fast."

"You must be wrong, our Claire wouldn't do a thing like that. She's not old enough to know anything about it, she doesn't have a boyfriend anyway. Have you spoken to her about it?"

"You're too old fashioned, Stan. Girls of fourteen these days know more about sex than we ever did. As far as we know she doesn't go out with a boy but there are plenty of them at school. It's illegal to have sex with a girl under sixteen but it doesn't stop them doing it. I haven't spoken to her yet, I was hoping she might come to me, but we can't leave it too much longer before we find out for sure. That's why I'm telling you now, what should we do?"

"We'll have it out with her when she gets home from school this afternoon. If she is pregnant there'll be hell to pay. We'll have to find out who's responsible and have it out with him and his parents. She's got all her life in front of her and her GCSE's next year! She doesn't want to be saddled with a kid at her age. We'll get to the bottom of this, and quickly."

"It's no use getting worked up, Stan. We don't know for sure yet and going at her like a bull in a china shop isn't going to help at all. You'd better leave it to me to speak to her. If she is pregnant she will be feeling lousy and riddled with guilt. She will need a lot of understanding from us."

"OK, you tackle her about it as soon as she gets home, I'll stay out of the way, but, if you're right, I want to know about it straight away and ask her some questions myself. All right, I'll treat her gently, don't worry, she's my little girl after all, probably been taken advantage of by some lout at school, I know what boys can be like at that age. I was one once."

At twenty past four that afternoon the front door opened and Claire walked in.

"I'm home mum!", she called out as she went up the stairs, "I'll be in my bedroom, I want to get this homework done out of the way."

Freda Hollingsworth wiped her hands, came out of the kitchen and followed her daughter up the stairs. She entered the bedroom, shut the door behind her, sat on the bed and motioned for Claire to sit beside her.

"What's up, mum?" asked Claire, "You look worried, has anything happened?"

"It's you I'm worried about, love. I think it's about time we had a little chat, don't you?"

"I don't know what you mean, mum. I haven't done anything. I really have got lots of homework to do this evening, can't this wait?"

"No, Claire, your homework can wait. I think you've got something to tell me. Come on, I won't be angry."

"I still don't know what you mean, mum, what's it all about?"

"All right, I was hoping you would trust me to understand and tell me yourself, but I'll ask you straight out. Are you pregnant?"

Claire burst into tears and cried, "I don't know, mum, I think I might be but I'm too frightened to find out."

Freda hugged her daughter saying, "You silly girl, why on earth didn't you say something? Haven't your dad and I always told you to tell us if anything is wrong? I've been watching you for the past couple of weeks, you haven't been right, then, this morning, when you were sick, I had to find out. We must take you round to the doctor's for a pregnancy test but, quite honestly, I don't think there's any doubt. We'll have to tell your dad."

"No, mum, please don't tell dad, not yet, he won't understand."

"I've already mentioned my suspicions to him, love, he's got to know. Don't worry, he'll be all right, you'll see. He loves you, you know that. We can't keep secrets from him, especially a thing like this. If we did he'd have every right to be angry. He wants to help you as much as I do. Come on, let's go downstairs and get it over with."

Stan Hollingsworth was sitting in the lounge watching television when his wife and daughter entered. At the look on their faces he switched off the set and sat back in his chair fearing the worst.

"I'm afraid it certainly looks as though I was right, Stan," said Freda Hollingsworth, "but we still don't know for sure. Claire has been too frightened to do anything about it, silly girl, but I'll take her to see the doctor this evening. She's feeling very ashamed of herself. I've told her you won't be angry with her."

Claire was sitting in an armchair opposite her father, head down, looking at the floor. The handkerchief in her hand was wet from the tears which were still flowing. She could not bring herself to look at him, steeling herself for the things she expected him to say.

Stan looked at his daughter trying desperately to keep hold of his emotions. It crossed his mind that this was something the parents of all teenaged girls dreaded most but it was no consolation to him. Why had it happened to his little girl? She was still not much more than a baby herself. There was plenty of time for this sort of thing later on in life. Why did kids have to experiment with sex? You couldn't really wonder at it when newspapers, magazines and television were throwing it at you all the time. He was trying hard to find the right words to say but, when he did speak, it was not what he intended to say.

"Who was it?" he asked, "Who's done this to you? I'll go straight round to his parents and have it out with them. Did he force himself on you?"

Claire did not answer, Freda signalled to him to tone it down a bit.

"Come on, Claire, who did this?", he repeated, "We've got to get to the bottom of it, you're not leaving here till we do."

"I can't tell you." whispered Claire, barely audible.

"What did you say?" asked her father, "I couldn't hear you, speak up."

"I can't tell you." repeated Claire, louder this time, "I knew it would be like this, why can't you leave me alone."

"It's no good behaving like that, Claire," said her mother, "we are only trying to help. Of course your father is upset, it has come as a shock to both of us. We've got to find out when it happened to see how far it's gone. You don't have to tell us who it was if you don't want to. If he's a decent young man he will tell us himself eventually. I don't suppose you've told him anything about it yet either, have you?"

"He can't be a decent young man!" retorted Stan Hollingsworth, "If he was he wouldn't have done this to you."

"I can't tell you anything." cried Claire, for the third time, "It's too late anyway, what's the point?"

"What do you mean, you can't tell us?" asked Stan letting his anger get the better of him, "Has there been more than one? Have you been at it so often you don't know who it is or when? I don't believe this! I thought I knew my daughter now I'm finding out she's a tart giving herself to anyone who wants it, at fourteen!"

Claire was sobbing into her handkerchief, still with head bent, not looking up at either of her parents.

"She doesn't mean that, Stan," said Freda, "You know only too well she's a good girl. Probably made just the one mistake and has been very unlucky. It happens. She obviously doesn't want the boy to get into trouble, she'll tell us who he is in good time, won't you, love?"

"I'll give him trouble when I get hold of him!", said Stan, "he's given us enough. A few minutes of pleasure and he's ruined her life. She'll have to get rid of it, she's far too young to be saddled with a kid."

"That's really up to Claire," said Freda, "I agree that an abortion is probably the best solution but she's got to have the final say. We don't even know for sure that she is pregnant yet. Let's leave any more discussion until after we've seen the doctor, she'll know best what to do. I'll ring the surgery now for an appointment."

Turning to Claire she said, "Go upstairs and get on with your homework, love, perhaps it will take your mind off it for a while. I'll let you know when it's time to go to the doctor's. Try to forget it for now. Your dad's not angry with you, you know. As I said, it has come as a shock and your dad finds it hard to control his feelings especially where you are concerned."

Claire wiped her eyes and made her way upstairs to her bedroom. She sat at the small desk in her room looking blankly at the school books in front of her. She had a huge feeling of relief that her secret was now out in the open but she couldn't help wishing that she could find the courage to tell her parents the truth.

Chapter fourteen

Detective Inspector Harty sat at his desk at West Town police station and studied his notes on the case so far. He was feeling just a little bit depressed. It was now Monday morning of the week after the robbery, five whole days had passed, and it seemed to him that they were still no nearer a solution. The Chief Superintendent was beginning to get impatient with the lack of progress and the Inspector knew that, if something positive didn't happen soon, the prospect of New Scotland Yard being called in was very real. He was anxious that that shouldn't happen, it had never been necessary before, in any case he had been involved in, he and his team had been able to solve them all unaided. He knew it was his past record that had persuaded the Chief Superintendent to hold off calling them in so far and he was determined to maintain that record. In this case, though, there had already been three murders, perhaps four with Jameson, and the pressure to find the killer quickly was greater than he had ever experienced before. If only they could trace Jameson, he thought, they might get the breakthrough they were looking for but, if Jameson were already dead, there was nobody else, as far as he was aware, who would be able to positively identify the killer.

He conceded that the man, Jimmy, if that was his real name, had done an excellent job in covering his tracks. The Inspector wondered if Jimmy was really that clever or was it simply that circumstances were helping him? No information at all had been forthcoming from the usual sources of informants which convinced the Inspector that Jimmy was not a habitual criminal but somebody who, up to now, had been a law abiding citizen and that the bus robbery was his first attempt at crime. The fact that Jimmy had enrolled three inexperienced youngsters for the job strengthened that theory, it was hardly the sort of thing a hardened criminal would do. If that was the case then what had caused the man to change? If shortage of money, perhaps fear of losing his home through non-payment of the mortgage, was the motive for the robbery, why the killings? If the reason for killing the youngsters was to avoid sharing the robbery proceeds, why kill the bus driver?

All these questions were going round in the Inspector's mind but, for the time being, he could find no reasonable answer to any of them. The most obvious explanation was the one that had struck him from the beginning and which still persisted, that the killer was somebody connected with the buses, the bus driver had recognised him and had therefore been shot, and the lads were killed simply to stop them talking if they were caught. Was there some other explanation? Was there something, quite fundamental, that they had so far overlooked? Whatever it was Inspector Harty was certain that Jimmy's luck could not hold out much longer. In his experience cleverness did not last for long. Sooner, rather than later, something would happen to point the finger. It had to, Jimmy was a very dangerous man.

As the Inspector got up from his desk he called out for Sergeant Tully, "Come on, Bob, we're going round to the bus depot. Bring DC Robson with you, he can go through the lockers there while we ask a few more questions."

"Won't we need a search warrant, Guv?" asked the Sergeant.

"I've got one, Bob, had it since first thing this morning."

The depot manager looked up from his desk and was surprised to see the three policemen as they walked into his office.

"I wasn't expecting to see you this morning, Inspector," he said, "I've had no message to say you were coming. Has there been a development? Have you come to arrest somebody?"

"No, that's just the point," replied the Inspector, "we seem to be getting nowhere at all and I'm convinced that someone here must know something. Most of the pointers we do have, and there aren't many, seem to indicate that the robbery was carried out by somebody who knew the bus route, the times of the buses and also had a very good idea of the passengers that particular bus would be carrying. I want to speak to everybody on duty here today and I want a list of those not on duty together with their addresses. I also want DC Robson, here, to look through the mens' lockers and anywhere else anything of any possible use to us may be kept. One of your men can go with him if you wish."

"I'm afraid that's not very convenient today," said the manager, "Monday's are very busy for us what with scheduling for the week and arranging cover for drivers off sick. We've got Thompson's funeral as well this week, that's taking a lot of arranging I can tell you. As for going through the lockers, they are the mens' personal property. I can't really allow that."

"I have a search warrant here," said the Inspector, handing it over to the manager, "and, as for the inconvenience, we have a dangerous killer to find. How inconvenient do you imagine it would be to his next victim and that victim's family? Believe me, this man won't stop at his young helpers, anyone who poses a threat to him and his freedom is in danger. If he is one of the men from here even you could be regarded as a threat for helping us, have you thought of that?"

The manager was visibly shaken at this last remark, it obviously hadn't occurred to him that he could be in danger.

"I take your point, Inspector," he said without further thought, "you can count on all the co-operation you need and for as long as it takes. Where do you want to start?"

"If you can arrange it so that the locker room is out of bounds until DC Robson has finished there it would be a big help. We don't want things taken from those lockers until they have been cleared."

"That's not going to be at all popular," said the manager, "but I'll arrange it straight away. Fred Dickens has half an hour free, I'll get him to help, we all know we can trust him. If the Detective Constable can have it done fairly quickly I would be very grateful. I'll fetch the duplicate keys for him."

Turning to the Constable the Inspector said, "OK Robson, you get on with that. The Sergeant and I will start with the maintenance crew. Come to us there immediately if you find anything worthwhile."

"By the way," he continued, this time to the manager, "are Hollingsworth and Davies on duty today?"

The manager consulted a chart on the wall and said, "Davies is here today but Hollingsworth won't be on until Wednesday, today and tomorrow are his rest days. Do you want me to call him in for you?"

"Good lord no, I'll see him at home if need be, along with the others after we've finished here. Make sure you have that list for me before we go. By the way, is Thompson's car still here?"

"No," replied the manager, "Mr Matthews called to collect it last Saturday morning, said he would try to sell it. He should get quite a good price for it I should think, it was in very good condition."

"That's life for you," said the Inspector, "there's always someone who benefits from somebody else's bad fortune. You mentioned Thompson's funeral just now, that's on Wednesday, isn't it?

"Yes, eleven-thirty Wednesday morning. Thompson was a bit of a loner as you know and, apart from Hollingsworth, hadn't many friends here even though he was one of our longest serving drivers, but a lot of the lads want to attend the funeral because of the way he died. A sort of, 'There, but for the grace of God' syndrome, I suppose. The Company are paying for it all as a tribute to him and to show, publicly, that they care about their staff."

"Where's it being held?"

"At St. Luke's in the High Street. The cortege is leaving Thompson's house at about ten-forty-five, his cousin, Mr Matthews is arranging that side of things. I'm expecting him here tomorrow morning to discuss the final details. It's a great pity Thompson had no close relations, if it wasn't for the lads here mourners at the funeral would be very thin on the ground."

"Is he being buried or cremated?" asked Detective Sergeant Tully.

"Cremated, Mr Matthews insisted on that, said he knew it was what Thompson would have wished. We would have preferred a burial, seems more appropriate under the circumstances somehow but we can't go against relations' wishes."

"We shall be there, at the crematorium, on Wednesday." said the Inspector, "Didn't know the chap, of course, but we feel closely involved. Come on, Bob, let's go and talk to the maintenance crew."

Harry Davies was working on an engine at the rear of a double decker bus when he saw the two policemen enter the maintenance area. He stopped what he was doing and from the pocket of his overalls took a piece of rag which he used to wipe his hands as he walked over to greet them.

"Hello Inspector, Sergeant," he said, "have you come to give us some good news? Have you caught Pete Thompson's killer yet?"

"Unfortunately not." replied Inspector Harty, "We're here to ask you and your mates some more questions. We've cleared it with the manager and, hopefully, the answers you give us may help to clear up one or two points for us. Let's start with you Mr Davies, perhaps you can tell us some more about the bus breakdown you attended last Tuesday afternoon."

"But I told you all there is to tell the other day, it was just a routine call out, a blown water hose that had to be replaced. It was on route fifty-one, a long way from the bus that was robbed. What's the problem?"

"You gave the impression, when you told us about it, that you worked on that job until it was finished." said the Inspector, "You made no mention of the fact that you had to return to the depot for a replacement part. Why was that?"

"I didn't think it was important." replied Davies, "I wasn't gone long, about ten minutes or so I suppose."

"That's not what the bus driver, Mr Dickens, has told us," said the Inspector, "he said you were gone for the best part of an hour, he wondered where you had got to."

"It probably did seem like an hour to him." Davies said, "He had nothing to do but wait, you know how time drags when you're waiting for someone. I just went straight back to the depot, picked up a spare water hose then returned to the bus and fitted it. What's all this leading to?"

"Mr Dickens was quite sure of the length of time you were away getting the part." the Inspector said, "He looked at his watch several times. He also said that you told him you had to go to central stores for the part as there was not one at the depot and that was why you had been away so long. What do you have to say about that?"

"Oh yes, that's right, it was that job," exclaimed Davies, looking decidedly worried, "I remember now. I came back to the depot first but there were no water hoses here. We had had a run on them, you see, that cold snap at the end of last month, I told you most of the buses here are on their last legs. The parts hadn't been restocked so I had to go over to central stores on the industrial estate to get one. Yes, thinking about it, I suppose it did take about an hour all told."

"Well, you must admit it's not very convincing, is it Mr Davies?" the Inspector replied, "You must seriously think of your position here. I trust that there is somebody to vouch for your story, you can be assured that we shall be making further enquiries as to your movements last Tuesday afternoon. If we find any more discrepancies your situation could be very grave. I have just one more question for you, where were you between three and six o'clock on Thursday afternoon?"

"Thursday was one of my rest days," replied Davies, "during the afternoon I was working on an Escort that had broken down in Twyford Road, over by the park. I finished it at about five thirty then went home for my tea."

"Twyford Road is near the South Gate entrance to the park, isn't it?" asked Detective Sergeant Tully.

"Yes, I believe it is." replied Davies with an air of resignation.

With that the Inspector and Sergeant left Harry Davies to carry on with his work while they questioned the rest of the maintenance crew.

Two hours later the three policemen met back in the manager's office having completed their task at the depot.

"Have you come up with anything new?" asked the manager putting his pen down on the papers he had been working on.

"No more than I expected." replied the Inspector giving absolutely nothing away. "You were certainly right about Thompson being a loner, nobody here seems to know anything much about him and they've apparently no idea what he got up to outside working hours. From what I had already heard from my earlier visits here and from you in particular, it confirms that point at least. It was the main reason I didn't carry out today's session sooner, no real point, you see, and we had more important things to follow through. There's nothing concrete, so far, to connect anyone here today with the robbery but we've got other avenues to follow, also there are still those off duty to see. Have you got that list for me?"

The manager handed him a list of names and addresses.

"Another reason for being here today," continued the Inspector, "is that most of the men here would not have been on duty last Tuesday when the robbery took place. It's very unlikely that, if our killer is a busman, he would have carried out the robbery during working hours unless he had a very valid reason for being out and about. A driver could not have left his bus without drawing attention to himself and anybody else would probably have been missed and we know that our man is doing all he can to avoid being identified, including bumping off all witnesses."

"I know all the lads here personally," said the manager, "and I would stake my life that none of them could be as callous as this man has been."

"You may wish you hadn't said that." said the Inspector meaningfully, then, turning to DC Robson, he asked, "Well, Robson, I take it there was nothing of interest in the lockers or anywhere else?"

"Nothing to do with this case, sir," replied Robson, "a few of the inevitable girlie mags and one or two items the manager here might be interested in but, otherwise, nothing. Thompson's locker was completely empty, by the way."

"I know," said the Inspector, "we took that lot away last Tuesday evening when we were here after the robbery."

To the manager he said, "Sorry to take up so much of your time this morning but, as you can appreciate, it was necessary. We shall leave you alone now and visit some of the people on this list, there's still a chance something useful may come to light."

As they left the bus depot the Inspector said to Detective Sergeant Tully, "We'll drop Robson off at the station, Bob, then pop round to Matthews's place before we see anyone else. It's common courtesy to let the man know we shall be at the funeral on Wednesday and, besides, there's something else I want to ask him."

"He may be at work, Guv," said the Sergeant, "wouldn't it be easier to ring?"

"We can take a chance on him being at home, we've got to go over that way anyway so there's no harm done."

As they turned into Thirston Close they saw the familiar blue and white gas company van outside number nine, pulled up behind it, got out and rang the front door bell.

The door was opened by Geoff Matthews. "Oh, hello Inspector," he said, "you've only just caught me. I've had a call to a job on the other side of town, can't hang on long, I'm afraid, got any news for me?"

"I won't take up much of your time," promised the Inspector, "I want to let you know that we shall be at your cousin's funeral on Wednesday. You don't object, do you?"

"Good heavens no, it's very kind of you, Inspector. Want to see if the killer turns up there I suppose, they say somebody who kills can't resist attending the funeral, don't they?"

"I wouldn't know, sir, we wouldn't know the killer if we saw him anyway, they usually don't look any different to anyone else, you know. By the way, we've found a certain amount of hard core pornographic material at your cousin's house, were you aware of it?"

"Porn? At Pete's? No, I know nothing about that, it's news to me. I find it hard to believe. He wasn't interested in women, I think I've already told you that."

"That's as may be, sir, but he had a number of very blue videos. I wondered if you may know where he got them?"

"I've no idea, Inspector, it sounds to me as if he was a bit of a dark horse, what else has he been up to?"

"We don't know yet, sir, but, in our experience, a man who says he is not interested in women, unless, of course he's gay, really means that women are not interested in him and therefore tries to get his kicks in other ways. Are you sure he never gave you any indication of what he got up to?"

"No, Inspector, as I've told you before, we didn't see him all that often and, when we did, he just came across as a nice, straightforward guy. Now, I must get moving or there will be hell to pay."

"Just one more question, sir, can you tell me where you were at about four thirty last Thursday?"

"Last Thursday, let me see, oh yes, I was here, mowing the grass out the back, I think. Can I go now?"

"Thank you, sir." said the Inspector.

When Matthews had gone Detective Sergeant Tully said, "Do you still suspect him, Guv? To my mind Davies is the far better bet."

"I've got an open mind, Bob, just exploring every channel. Davies, Matthews and Hollingsworth are still the only possible suspects we have but, I must admit, I can't think of any motive any of them could have had for staging that robbery, apart from the obvious which would include almost anybody in the country. Let's pop round to Hollingsworth and see what he has to say for himself."

Stan Hollingsworth was just about to go upstairs when the front door bell rang. He gave a tut of annoyance and opened the door to find the two policemen standing there.

"Oh, it's you again, is it," he said, "what do you want this time? I don't suppose you've caught Pete's murderer yet."

"No, I'm afraid we haven't." replied Detective Inspector Harty, "We've just spent a couple of hours or so at the bus depot and are following it up by calling on the rest of you who are off duty today. It shouldn't take long, may we come in?"

"I suppose so," replied Hollingsworth, opening the door wide for them, "although I can't see that I can tell you any more than I have already."

"Well, one or two things have come to light since we last saw you and we would like clarification on a couple of points. You, or your wife, told us that Thompson was not much of a one where women are concerned, is that right?"

"Yes, that's right. Since his wife left him all those years ago he's hardly been out with anyone else. He had a couple of dates to my knowledge, perhaps five in all certainly no more, over a period of three years following his divorce, but none of them went any further than that. Just the one evening with each of them then nothing, he just couldn't get along with them. Said he was happier with his own company and didn't want to get involved with anyone else. Why do you ask?"

"Did you know that Thompson was into pornography?" asked the Inspector.

"Pete? You must be joking. He didn't even like a smutty story. Went as red as a beetroot whenever anyone told one."

"We've found quite a number of hard porn videos in his house," said Detective Sergeant Tully, "all disguised as something else quite innocent. Are you sure you weren't aware they were there?"

"Of course I'm sure," Hollingsworth replied, "and, knowing Pete as I did, I can't believe they were his. If they were his I'm sure he would have told me, he knew I enjoy a bit of that myself now and again."

"Oh, they were his all right," said the Sergeant, "they were all catalogued on his computer. He knew precisely where each one was and what it contained. He also knew how often each one had been seen and on what dates."

"The old so-and-so," remarked Hollingsworth, "talk about a dark horse! It just goes to show that you don't really know anybody, doesn't it, however well you think you do."

"Exactly," replied the Inspector, "now perhaps you can understand a little of what we're up against and why we must continue to ask you, and others, these questions.

Every answer we get helps to fit the jigsaw together just a little bit more."

"I can't see how knowing Pete was into porn helps with solving the reason for the robbery and his murder." said Hollingsworth, "I would say that a very high proportion of men watch blue movies but they don't all go and get robbed and murdered."

"Statistics show that not as many watch them as you might think." said the Inspector, "But that's not the point. At the moment we don't know the true motive for the bus hold up. I don't think it was purely for money, and, quite honestly, I don't really think that Thompson's murder was a spontaneous act. The more information we have on the backgrounds of the people involved, and those around them, the better chance we have of reaching a solution."

"I can see what you mean," replied Hollingsworth, "the sooner you find who did it the better, as far as I'm concerned."

"Can you tell me where you were at about four thirty last Thursday afternoon?" asked Inspector Harty.

"That was out of the blue!" exclaimed Hollingsworth, "Let me see, of course, I was driving the number thirty-seven bus, just dropped off a crowd of kids from the secondary school, rowdy lot they are.

"Right, thank you Mr Hollingsworth, that will be all for now. We shall see you at the funeral on Wednesday. I expect you will be glad when that's over?"

"You'll be there too?" asked Hollingsworth, "Yes, I suppose that makes sense."

The two policemen said no more but made their way to the car and continued with the interviews of others on the list supplied by the depot manager.

Chapter fifteen

Detective Inspector Harty and Detective Sergeant Tully walked into West Town police station discussing the fruitless visits they had just been engaged on. Very little additional information had been gained during the three hours of interviews with the bus company employees on the list they had been given but, as they reflected, that was typical of ninety percent of their job. As they passed through the main office the duty sergeant approached them.

"Mr Watkins, the newsagent manager, is waiting to see you sir." he said to the Inspector.

"Oh good, has he been waiting long?" asked Inspector Harty.

"About fifteen minutes. I told him that I wasn't sure when you would be back but he insisted on waiting, said it was urgent."

"OK, give me three minutes to get settled then send him in to my office."

"I wonder if he's got some new information for us, Bob," he said turning to Sergeant Tully, "I'm sure there's more he can tell us about what happened last Tuesday."

"Let's hope so, Guv," replied Sergeant Tully, "we can certainly do with something to be getting on with. Perhaps it won't be a completely wasted day after all."

A few minutes later Peter Watkins was shown into the Inspector's office. As he walked through the doorway Inspector Harty, who was now seated at his desk, looked up at him and smiled a welcome.

"Ah, Mr Watkins," he said, "I believe you have been waiting for me, something urgent I'm told, please take a seat."

The Inspector gestured towards a chair in front of his desk. Detective Sergeant Tully was already seated at one side of the room holding a note pad in his lap and a pencil in his hand.

"Well, Inspector," said Peter Watkins, "I thought I had better come along as soon as I found out. You, or rather the Sergeant here, told me to keep you informed if anything came to light and I think that what I have to tell you is very important."

"Very good," said the Inspector, "we can do with all the information we can get. Sergeant Tully will take notes, I'm sure you won't mind. Now, what is it you have to tell me?"

"I found out only this morning, from one of my regular customers, that last Tuesday afternoon, the day of the robbery, just after I left the shop to go to the bank, my assistant, George Butler, made a call from the public telephone box outside the post office which is next door but one from the shop. The call didn't take long apparently, but the customer mentioned it because he said he thought it was odd that George should use that box when there's a 'phone in the shop."

"And what significance do you put on this?" asked the Inspector while glancing across at Sergeant Tully who had shifted his position and was looking at Watkins with renewed interest.

"Well, don't you see!" exclaimed Peter Watkins, "He must have been giving the gang the message that I was on the way and telling them which bus I was on. What else could it be? I must say, though, that I would never have believed it of George. He's been with me for over four years now and I'd grown to trust him completely. It goes to show that you can't really trust anybody these days, doesn't it? Another thing, he was on his own that afternoon and he shouldn't have left the shop unattended even for a short while."

"It's just possible you are doing him an injustice," said the Inspector, "but, I must admit, it does sound suspicious. Have you asked him about it?"

"No, Inspector, I haven't said anything at all to him. I thought I'd better let you know about it first. That's why I came straight round here, I didn't want to frighten him off or anything. You know how to handle these things much better than I do."

"Good, you did the right thing there, we'll come round to the shop and ask some questions. You get back there now, Mr Watkins, and please act perfectly naturally but don't tell him where you've been. We'll follow on a little bit later, we don't want to arouse his suspicions by suddenly turning up all together. By the way, I suppose the customer who told you this is reliable?"

"He's been coming to the shop for a few years now, lives just around the corner. I can't see why he would want to make up a story like that, besides, he only really mentioned it in passing. He said he didn't want to get George into trouble but it puzzled him to see George in the 'phone box."

"I just wonder why he didn't mention it sooner?" remarked the Inspector, "Still, late is better than not at all. O.K. Mr Watkins, thank you for coming round, we'll call in at the shop in about an hour or so."

As Peter Watkins went out of the door Inspector Harty said to Sergeant Tully, "You realise, of course, Bob, that if Watkins is right and Butler did call the gang from that 'phone box then he must know who our man is. This could be the break we're looking for. There's just one thing that bothers me though, and I'm sure you know what it is."

"Yes, Guv, knowing the way the killer thinks, as I believe we do by now, if Butler was involved enough to telephone him about the trip to the bank then, by right, he should be dead."

"Exactly, Bob, that's why I'm not reading too much into this at this stage, but it could be the killer's first big mistake. Let's hope so. We should soon know one way or the other."

As the two policemen entered the newsagents in Wirral Road the manager, Peter Watkins, was poring over the books containing details of newspaper deliveries and payments due while his assistant was serving the only customer in the shop. They browsed through the magazines until the customer had gone then approached the manager who greeted them as if it was the first time he had seen them that day.

"Mr Watkins," said the Inspector loud enough for the assistant to hear clearly what was said, "we would like to ask some more questions concerning the money that was taken from you during that robbery last week. Perhaps your assistant here would like to speak to Detective Sergeant Tully while I'm talking to you, that would save time. I see you're not too busy at the moment."

"No we are not, Inspector," replied the manager, "this time of the day is always quiet, that would be fine."

Turning to his assistant he said, "George, this is Detective Inspector Harty and Detective Sergeant Tully. They are looking into the robbery on that bus last week when the driver was killed and our money taken. Tell the Sergeant everything you can, don't hold anything back, the sooner this case is settled the better, eh Inspector?"

George Butler was a pleasant looking young man of twenty-four. He was prematurely balding from the forehead but this didn't detract from his boyish good looks. He was wearing a white shirt with a plain light blue tie, and grey flannel trousers. He looked eminently respectable and gave the impression of enjoying his job.

"Mr Butler," said Detective Sergeant Tully, "I wonder if you can tell me anything you can remember about last Tuesday afternoon. Take your time and think carefully, something that may seem trivial to you could be important to us. I don't want to put words into your mouth."

"I don't think there's very much at all I can tell you," replied Butler, "I do remember that it was a very quiet afternoon, very few customers. We get most of our customers first thing in the morning, late afternoon and evening and during the lunch hour, you see. Our busiest times are when the kids go to school and then again when they go home."

"I would like you to concentrate mainly on the period between two and four o'clock of that afternoon." said the Sergeant, "Anything that you, or anyone else perhaps, did out of the ordinary."

"Well, Mr Watkins left here to go to the bank with the money from the tills just before two o'clock but that's what he usually does. I was shocked when I heard what had happened on the bus. I was wondering where on earth he had got to, he was usually back soon after three but it was nearly five before he got back that afternoon. I had finished the papers for the evening rounds by then."

Sergeant Tully realised that here was a young man who tended to ramble a bit and took his time coming to the point. Of course, he could be trying to avoid mentioning anything about what he, himself, had been up to that afternoon but the Sergeant decided to give him the benefit of the doubt and let him carry on, for the time being, at his own pace although the odd prompt here and there wouldn't hurt.

"What did you do after Mr Watkins left the shop?" he asked.

"Let me think. As I said it was a very quiet afternoon. I served a lady customer with a bar of chocolate and a magazine soon after Mr Watkins left, the rest of the time I spent restocking the shelves, sorting out the old magazines and then preparing the evening paper rounds. I don't remember anything out of the ordinary in the shop that afternoon, of course I didn't know what was happening to Mr Watkins all that time and I was getting worried as the time wore on."

"Did you leave the shop at all during that afternoon?"

"No, I had no reason to. Besides there's nobody else here to take over. I would lose my job if I left the place unattended."

"Think again, Mr Butler. We have been told that you were seen in the public call box outside soon after Mr Watkins had gone, is that right?"

Butler's face turned as red as a beetroot and he started to stammer.

"I, I had forgotten about that, yes, I, I'm sorry, I did. But it only took a moment and I could see the shop the whole time. I would have known if anyone went in."

"Who did you call on the telephone? Now think carefully this time, it's very important."

"I 'phoned the betting shop in the High Street. My mother wanted me to place a bet for her on a horse in the three o'clock race at Cheltenham. It's a weakness of hers, I don't like doing it but she gets quite angry if I won't. I, I live with her you see."

"Why didn't you use the 'phone in the shop? Surely it would have been easier to do so?"

"Mr Watkins would have done his nut! He keeps a very tight control over all the calls made from that 'phone. It's not his fault, head office insist on a detailed listing of every outgoing call. They'd be down on him like a ton of bricks if anything other than business calls were made, especially calls to a betting shop, he'd probably lose his job. I wasn't out of the shop for long, about three minutes I suppose, and, as I said, I was watching it all the time, nobody went in or out."

"Why didn't your mother place the bet herself?"

"She's useless on the 'phone, gets very flustered, and she can't get out of the house to go to the betting shop herself. She's in a wheelchair you see. She finds out what races are going to be on television then picks a horse and bets on it. She watches the race and, if her horse wins, it makes her day. It's the only bit of pleasure she gets so I can't really refuse. I hope I'm not going to get the sack over it. I don't know what I'd do if that happens."

"That's not up to me," said Sergeant Tully, "but I'll have to check out your story, what was the name of the horse and how much was staked?"

"Two pounds each way on Naughty-but-Nice."

"And was it placed in the name of Butler?"

"Yes."

The Sergeant took out his two-way radio and contacted the station. "Get in touch with the bookmakers in the High Street," he said, "and check on a possible bet placed there, by 'phone, under the name of Butler, last Tuesday afternoon. Get back to me as soon as you've got an answer."

"Yes, Sarge," said the voice at the other end, "someone forget to pick up their winnings?"

"Cut out the funny stuff and get on with it. I need an answer straight away."

"While we're waiting for them to call back," said the Sergeant to George Butler, "can you tell me, by any chance do you know of either Frank Prescott, Phil Jameson or Tim Priestley?"

"Frank Prescott was that lad who was found in the burnt out Astra last week wasn't he? That was dreadful.

And Tim Priestley was found dead in the park. I read about them in the papers. Anything to do with the bus robbery is very interesting to me, after all Mr Watkins was involved in that and, when it happens to someone you know, it's almost like being involved yourself. I didn't know of them before reading of their deaths. What was the other name you mentioned?"

"Phil Jameson."

"No, I don't know anyone of that name either."

At that moment the Sergeant's radio came to life. "Checked with the bookmakers, Sarge," said the voice, "a bet was placed over the 'phone at five past two last Tuesday afternoon, in the name of Butler, two pounds each way on Naughty-but-Nice in the three o'clock at Cheltenham, 'fraid it came in fifth, can't win 'em all!"

"Well, you heard that," Sergeant Tully said to George Butler, "it certainly confirms what you told me. I don't think there's anything else to ask you at the moment but if you do think of anything that may help us don't hesitate to let us know."

"Yes, Sergeant, I certainly will. I'm sorry I forgot to mention that 'phone call it had honestly gone out of my mind."

Detective Inspector Harty took his leave of Peter Watkins and, together, he and Detective Sergeant Tully left the shop.

Outside, the Sergeant said, "Well, Guv, another dead end it seems, I really thought we might be getting somewhere at last."

"Yes, Bob," replied the Inspector, "but doesn't it occur to you that your interview with Butler was far from conclusive. O.K. a call he made at five past two has been confirmed as to the bookmaker to place a bet but who is to say that it was the call made from the call box or, if it was, that he didn't make more than one call. We've only got his word for it and there's no way, that I can see, that we can confirm it one way or the other. Is Mr Butler being very clever or do we take him at face value?"

"He certainly seems an honest enough young chap," replied Sergeant Tully, "I'm afraid I'm inclined to believe him. Mr Watkins has said that he has found him to be completely trustworthy over four years and we certainly have nothing at all on him. It's easy enough to forget something like a 'phone call over the period of a week."

I don't know, Bob. I'm still not convinced. He went behind Watkins' back to make that 'phone call and left the shop unattended while he did. Hardly completely trustworthy, I'd say. Although, as we've already remarked, if he does know the killer and was involved in any way with the robbery why is he still alive? Unless, for some reason, the killer finds him completely trustworthy too. I think we'll just have to wait and see."

Chapter sixteen

It was now Tuesday morning of the week following the raid on the bus on route thirty-seven. Seven days had passed since the robbery and the brutal killing of driver Pete Thompson. It seemed to Detective Inspector Harty that a solution to the case was as far away as ever. If only Jameson would turn up alive and well. Then perhaps they could make some constructive moves. Inspector Harty, however was a positive thinker and his unshakeable optimism had always held him in good stead. He saw no real reason why it should be any different in this case. Generally speaking the criminal fraternity were a vain lot and always believed they were one better than the police. More often than not they were too clever, or thought they were, for their own good and, sooner or later, would make the inevitable mistake which would lead to their downfall. As he had said to Detective Sergeant Tully the previous afternoon, after the interview with Butler at the newsagents, perhaps this one had already made his mistake, only time would tell. He had solved much more complicated cases than this one in the past and one of them in particular had taken months of investigation before proof was finally established.

It was lack of evidence and especially the lack of an apparent motive, apart from robbery, that made this one different. The Inspector had not come up against anybody before who had covered his tracks as completely as this man Jimmy had appeared to have done. It was that more than anything else that he found so frustrating. Every possible lead so far had petered out rather rapidly leaving them floundering at the same dead end. There had to be a common factor somewhere, some missing link that would complete the chain and lead them in the right direction. The Inspector was still convinced, in his own mind, that Jameson was probably that missing link or, at the very least, the means of finding it. He had to be found soon, and alive! If he were already dead and buried or his body hidden somewhere then, at the moment, the Inspector had no idea what the next move could be to find Jimmy. Jimmy? That very probably wasn't his name anyway. They had not found any known Jim's or Jimmy's within the scope of their investigations into this crime, and every one of the off-duty men from the depot had alibis for last Tuesday afternoon. As the Inspector himself had said earlier the name Jimmy is widely used by people casually addressing someone they do not know by name. It was very unlikely that the instigator of the bus robbery had come from another area, he was almost definitely a local man who had hired local boys to do his dirty work. No, the Inspector was convinced that the man lived in or around the town and was still there, and that he either knew somebody who worked on the buses or worked there himself, nothing had happened, so far, to alter that viewpoint.

"We must follow up on that story the newsagent's assistant, Butler, gave us, Bob." he said, shaking himself free from the line of thought that had been passing through his mind, "I agree with you that he seems to be a very plausible fellow and the story he told could very well be true but, as I said yesterday, there are too many loose ends."

"We've been on to British Telecom, Guv, to see if they can help," replied Detective Sergeant Tully, "but it seems that a week is too long to trace back on calls from public call boxes so we still don't know for sure whether he made more than one call or not that afternoon. I also got a list of the calls from the shop 'phone from Mr

Watkins, there were none at all during Tuesday afternoon. B.T. were able to confirm that."

"Even if there was more than one call from the 'phone box, Bob, we couldn't prove that Butler had made it. Anybody could have used that box during the afternoon. We shall have to think up a way of getting more information from him, let him think we are happy with what he has told us and try to catch him unawares. Of course, if he is telling us the truth that won't do us any good anyway but it's worth a try. It would be an idea to find out if he has any connection at all to Hollingsworth, Davies or Matthews. I'm still unhappy about those three."

"I can make a habit of calling in there for my morning paper if you like," said Sergeant Tully, "it's not far out of my way and I can pass the odd pleasantry with Butler, get him used to seeing me there. In that way perhaps he'll let something slip, if there is anything to slip. At any rate it'll give me a chance to find out a little more about him and see whether my first impressions were right."

"Sounds like a good idea, Bob, we might be clutching at straws but, if I'm right, he probably knows rather more than he's telling us."

Detective Constable Robson tapped on the door at that point and walked into the office.

"Uniform have brought in somebody you might like to see, Guv," he said, addressing the Inspector, "a young lad, about seventeen or eighteen, I'd say, been living rough and in quite a state. He refuses to give his name, or any other information, but bears a striking resemblance to the photograph of Jameson you released last week. At least, if you ignore the filth on his face you would certainly say it was him."

Inspector Harty and Sergeant Tully looked at each other expectantly.

"Where is he?" asked the Inspector.

"They've put him in number two interview room," replied Robson, "but he could do with a good scrub and a change of clothes. It's not going to be very pleasant in there until he's been cleaned up."

"Did he have anything on him?"

"A couple of quid, a small bunch of keys and a handkerchief, that's all."

"If it is Jameson I wonder what he's done with the money?" asked Sergeant Tully.

"He's hardly likely to carry that much around with him if he's living rough." said the Inspector. "That would be asking for trouble. He's probably hidden it somewhere unless, of course, it's already been taken from him."

"Well, we can be quite sure it wouldn't have been taken by Jimmy," said the Sergeant, "otherwise it would have been another corpse they'd brought in."

"You are probably right," said Inspector Harty, "let's go and see him."

As they entered the interview room they saw at once that the lad was indeed in a state. Looking at him the Inspector thought that living rough was putting it mildly, he had seen his fair share of down-and-outs in his time but none of them matched this one.

"Where on earth did they find him?" he asked D.C.Robson.

"He was at the north end of the landfill sight at the edge of town. A couple of the drivers of the Corporation dust carts that dump their rubbish there spotted him. The site foreman reported it to the police."

"We're not going to get much from him while he's in that state." said the Inspector, "He probably feels that the whole world's against him at the moment and I doubt that he's had a decent meal for a week. Take him to get cleaned up then to the canteen for something to eat. Give him whatever he wants. We'll see him after that, let us know when he's ready."

As D.C.Robson led the lad away the Inspector said to Sergeant Tully, "Well, Bob, I don't think there's much doubt that's Jameson and at least he's alive. Maybe things will start improving now."

An hour and a half later Detective Inspector Harty and Detective Sergeant Tully were back in number two interview room facing a much more respectable young man. He was wearing a white tee shirt and blue jeans donated from one of the police lockers and was certainly looking happier and much more comfortable than at their first meeting.

"Now," said the Inspector, "this is a completely informal interview at this stage. You are not under arrest, nothing will be recorded on tape and there's no need to mention solicitors. We need to establish who you are, where you live and what you were doing at the place you were found. First of all, what is your name?"

The young man did not answer.

"Keeping silent will not help you at all. As I said, this is completely informal, what you say at the moment is between you, me and the Sergeant here. I repeat, nothing is being recorded. Later, if necessary and if you turn out to be who we think you are, you may be cautioned and then you will not be obliged to say anything, you may also have a lawyer present, if you wish, but at the moment we simply need to establish certain facts. Now, what is your name?"

"Jameson, Philip Jameson," whispered the lad, almost inaudibly.

"Could you speak a little louder!"

"Philip Jameson."

"And how old are you?"

"Eighteen".

"Where do you live?"

"Nowhere now!"

"What do you mean by that?"

"I used to live with a friend but he's not around any more. My dad kicked me out of home when I left school. He never did like me."

"Am I right in thinking that the friend you lived with was Frank Prescott?" asked the Inspector quietly. He saw Jameson's shoulders droop and a very pained expression cross his face as he obviously relived the horror he had seen.

"Yes, Frankie was the best friend anyone could have, now he's gone and it's all my fault. It was horrible. Why did I have to get him involved?"

Inspector Harty looked across at Sergeant Tully and said to Jameson, "Before you say anything else I think we have now come to the point where I must caution you. This interview is no longer informal but official and everything said in this room from now on will be recorded." He nodded to the Sergeant who switched on the machine then continued, "This is an interview between Detective Inspector Edward Harty and the suspect, Philip Jameson, timed at fifteen-twenty-two on Tuesday, 14th of May. Also present is Detective Sergeant Robert Tully.

"Philip Jameson, I have reason to believe that you were involved in the waylaying and robbery of a number thirty-seven bus on the afternoon of Tuesday, 7th May. You do not have to say anything. It may harm your defence if you do not mention something when questioned that you later rely on in court. Anything you say will be taken down and may be used in evidence. Do you understand?"

Jameson nodded assent.

"Do you understand? Please answer for the recorder."

"Yes, I understand. It's a relief to talk after what's happened over the past few days. I'd like to tell you all I can."

"It's your right to have a lawyer present if you wish." said the Inspector.

"I don't need a lawyer, I'll tell you all I know. The bus robbery seemed like a lark at first. I was desperate for money and it seemed like a good way of getting it, with a bit of adventure thrown in. I hadn't been able to pay any rent to Frank for weeks and he had just been made redundant, it just didn't seem fair."

"How were you approached about the robbery?" asked Sergeant Tully.

"I was in the job centre in the High Street looking through the job cards when this bloke came up to me and said he had a job I might be interested in."

"When was this?" asked the Inspector.

"It seems like months ago but it was last Wednesday week, about half past ten."

"Did you know this man?"

"No, I'd never seen him before."

"How old was he? Can you describe him?"

"I don't know, about fifty I suppose, He was quite a big bloke, wore a duffle coat, looked like a builder or something."

"Did he tell you his name?"

"No, later on, when we were all together, he told us to call him Jimmy. I don't know if it was really his name or not, Jimmy is just an ordinary name isn't it? He looked sort of ordinary."

"What happened after he offered you the job?"

"He didn't tell me what the job was at first but said there could be a lot of money in it for me. He asked me if I knew anyone else who might be interested and I said

145

yes, thinking of Frankie. He told me to bring Frankie along to the library on Thursday evening when he would give us more details."

"Did he know your name?"

"Not until I told him. As I said I'd never seen him before. Frankie was a bit suspicious when I told him about it but we were both out of work so he couldn't see any harm in going along to find out more about it."

"What happened on the Thursday evening?"

"Well, me and Frankie went to the library and the bloke was there with somebody else, about the same age as us. He told us the other boy's name was Tim and would be doing the job with us. He told Tim our first names and it was at this point that he told us to call him Jimmy. We asked him what the job was and he told us it was something he had wanted to do for a long time but hadn't had the chance to do before. We couldn't believe it at first when he said we would be holding up a bus. We thought he was joking but he said no, he was serious. Frankie was all for leaving there and then but Jimmy was very persuasive and said there was no risk to us, it was all a big laugh really, part of a rag day stunt or something. He made it sound as if it was all a big game."

"What happened next?" asked Sergeant Tully.

"He told us to meet him again on Friday evening, this time at the Golden Goose pub, to go over what each of us would be doing. Frankie didn't want to go, said it all sounded very iffy, but I kept on to him until he gave in. Then, after that, we met again on Monday evening, the day before the robbery, at the Dog and Hounds when Jimmy issued us all with guns and duffle coats and scarves."

"What! He gave you those at the Dog and Hounds? It's a wonder nobody saw you." said the Inspector.

"Actually he gave them to us in a quiet corner of the car park after we'd been in the pub. He took them out of the boot of his car. All this time we thought it was nothing more than a lark, Jimmy had convinced us it was all part of a stunt, something to do with a charity, we thought, although he hadn't actually said so. When we got home Frankie soon discovered that the guns weren't real, although they looked good, and this really convinced us that Jimmy was telling the truth about it being a lark. By this time we were quite looking forward to it all, if only we'd known!"

"Can you remember what make of car Jimmy had in that car park?"

"It was the same one we used the following day after the hold up. The one Frankie was killed in, a Vauxhall Astra."

"How was it decided which bus to hold up?" asked the Inspector, "Did somebody else somewhere ring through at any time to say which bus it should be?"

"No," said Jameson, "Jimmy told us on Monday evening that it would be that particular bus, all part of the game, you see. We had to meet together at the bus stop there, but not all at once, between twenty past and twenty five past two. Jimmy seemed to get a bit worried when two women turned up as well."

"Well, that lets Butler out of the bag." the Inspector said to Sergeant Tully, "You were right, Bob, he must have been telling the truth all along. It also means that Jimmy, or whatever his name is, must have known, or at least had a good idea, who was going to be on that bus. As I thought, he must have some connection with the buses somewhere."

"It certainly looks like it, Guv," said Sergeant Tully, "perhaps Jameson here will be able to identify him for us at Thompson's funeral tomorrow. If Jimmy is on the buses he won't be able to resist attending. I've never known a killer yet who didn't want to see the thing through to the end."

Turning back to Jameson the Inspector said, "The newsagent, Peter Watkins, has told us that you seemed to know that he was carrying money in a bag under his coat. Is that right? I am right in thinking that you are the one who took it from him?"

"Yes," said Jameson, "Jimmy had told us that one of the male passengers would be carrying money in a special belt and that it was this money that he was really interested in. He told us that this man would be expecting us to take the belt but that we were to go through the motions of robbing all the other passengers to make it look authentic. He said that he didn't know where on the bus the passenger would be but he gave us quite a good description of him. I didn't know he was a newsagent. As it happens he was on the upper deck where I had the job of taking the money while Tim stood at the front covering the passengers with his gun."

"At what stage did you realise that the hold-up wasn't a game but the real thing?"

"Well, when I saw the look of horror on the passengers' faces when it all started I began to wonder. They all seemed too surprised, especially the one with the belt. If they knew what was coming they wouldn't all have acted as they did. Then there were two shots downstairs, I don't know what happened but I looked at Tim and he was scared out of his wits but it was too late to back out now. We finished with the passengers as quickly as possible then ran down the stairs and out to the car. I started the engine for a quick getaway, as Jimmy had told me to, then got into the back with Tim to wait for the others. We were looking out of the rear window and saw Frankie running towards us then we saw Jimmy shoot the bus driver in the head. We knew then, once and for all, that it was all for real."

"What happened after that?"

"Frankie was driving the car and Jimmy was sitting next to him. Frankie was obviously scared and wanted to get away as quickly as possible but Jimmy kept on to him to drive normally. When we got to some traffic lights he had to stop. I jumped out of the car and ran across the road, Tim did the same but went the other way. I expected Jimmy to come after me but he didn't."

"What made you run off like that? Was it because you had most of the money?"

"I didn't know what I had at that point, it was a spur of the moment thing, seemed like the best thing to do. I didn't like leaving Frankie like that but he didn't have much choice being in the driving seat, especially with Jimmy sitting next to him with a gun he had already used on somebody else."

"Where did you go when you ran from the car?"

"I went to the waste ground by the railway where Jimmy had said we would be paid after doing the job."

"Wasn't that a pretty stupid thing to do considering the circumstances?"

"I wanted to see if there was anything I could do to help Frankie, I had got him into this mess, I couldn't desert him could I? I didn't go straight to the building Jimmy had mentioned. I stayed hidden and crept up behind some old railway sleepers. Just as I got there I heard a shot and knew then I was too late to help Frankie but I didn't expect to see what Jimmy did to him, it was horrible."

At this point Jameson started to break down, his voice getting softer and tears welling up in his eyes. The two policemen looked at each other knowing what the lad was going through but they had to be sure about what had happened. Jameson was giving them a very clear picture of the events of that day, up to now a lot of it had been speculation, he was filling in a large piece of the jigsaw for them. The Inspector gently urged him on.

"You're doing very well lad," he said, "take your time, there's plenty to spare. When you are ready tell us just what Jimmy did to Frank. From your evidence we can build up a pretty hefty case against him."

Jameson cleared his throat and took a drink from a glass of water on the table. "I shudder every time I think about it. I just hope Frankie was already dead from that gunshot, I'm pretty sure he was I couldn't see any movement at all. Jimmy fetched a couple of petrol cans from out of the building and sprinkled petrol all over Frankie and the car then set it alight. It went up like a bomb. I'll never forget that sight as long as I live, it was awful. Why did he have to do it? Why did he kill Frankie? It doesn't make sense."

"Whatever the reason we'll find out, don't worry," said the Inspector, "now, what did Jimmy do after that?"

"I don't really know, he went off somewhere I think. I was too stunned to notice much, I just couldn't believe what was happening. I stayed behind the sleepers for what seemed like ages before I could make myself move."

"Where did you go when you left that place?"

"Well, I sat there thinking. I was going back to the flat but after what Jimmy did to Frankie I didn't feel safe any more, he knew where I lived and I thought he had probably gone there to find me. It was no good going to my mum and dad, especially now, they had made it clear they didn't want to know if I got into trouble so I decided to go to my aunt Audrey."

"But you didn't get there, did you?"

"No, on the way there I thought I had better get rid of the stuff from the robbery, and the coat and scarf. I dumped them in a dustbin down an alleyway by some shops. While I was doing that I thought about aunt Audrey and what she would do. She's very nice but she would have made me give myself up. I wouldn't have been able to tell her any lies, she always knows when I'm lying."

"The stuff in the dustbin was found and brought to us," said Sergeant Tully, "but there was no cash, there must have been some cash. You have just told us yourself that you were the one who robbed the newsagent, Mr Watkins. What did you do with it?"

"I kept the cash so that I could buy some food. I didn't know where I was going after I decided not to go to aunt Audrey's. The only place I could think of where Jimmy probably wouldn't think to look for me was at the back of the rubbish dump. That's where I've been ever since. It was horrible, I'm glad it's over now."

"How did you manage to buy food in the filthy state you were in?" asked the Sergeant, "Nobody in their right mind would serve you, they would probably have called us."

"I bought some tins, beans mostly, and a tin opener and some fruit on that first day. That lasted a few days. I didn't know what to do when I realised how dirty I was. I was trying to look round for ideas when I was caught today."

"What about the newsagent's money? The money in the special bag?" asked Inspector Harty, "What did you do with that."

"I've hidden it. It was a shock when I saw how much was there. I didn't want to carry that around with me in case Jimmy did find me so I hid it."

"Where?"

Jameson remained silent. He had already decided, in his own mind, that he deserved to keep the money after what he had been through.

"All right," said the Inspector, "play it your way for now, we'll come back to that later. Did you see anything more of Tim Priestley after you ran off from the car?"

"No, he went in the opposite direction. I hope he's all right, I didn't know his name was Priestley we only knew him as Tim."

"You don't know then that he has been killed too?"

"No! I didn't! That means I'm the only one left! How was he killed? The same as Frankie?"

"No, he was stabbed, found in the park a couple of days later, but we're pretty sure he was killed by Jimmy. It's the only possibility that makes sense. Jimmy must be getting pretty desperate to find you by now. I think you'll find this is the safest place for you for the time being."

"Can you tell us anything at all about Tim Priestley?" asked Detective Sergeant Tully.

"Not much, as I've said, I didn't really know him at all. The first time we met him was when Jimmy brought him along that first evening, we assumed he was a relation or something. Suppose he couldn't have been if Jimmy killed him, he wouldn't kill a relation like that, would he?"

"When somebody gets to the state of mind that Jimmy has reached anything's possible believe me!" Inspector Harty retorted, "That's why we must have him under lock and key as soon as possible. Having you here at last is a big bonus, you can obviously identify him for us, that is something he is desperate for you not to do. As far as we are aware you are now the only one who can do that and, until he is caught, you are in grave danger wherever you are."

"Interview terminated at sixteen-thirty-five." continued the Inspector switching off the recorder and turning to Sergeant Tully, "Jameson has done us proud, Bob, I think that's enough for now. Get his statement typed up and let him read it and sign it when it's done. Take him down to the cells and get the doctor to look him over, goodness knows what he may have picked up from that rubbish tip."

Chapter seventeen

I don't want the media knowing about Jameson yet, Bob." said Detective Inspector Harty as Detective Sergeant Tully returned from the cells. "In fact the fewer people who know he is here the better. If Jimmy gets word that we have Jameson he might go into hiding and it'll be harder still finding him. If he thinks Jameson is still out there somewhere he's going to carry on looking for him and while he's doing that we have a far better chance."

"But the papers already know somebody was found at the rubbish tip." said Sergeant Tully.

"Yes, but they don't know who he is. As far as they are concerned at the moment he was just a vagrant causing a nuisance and brought in for his own safety. They may suspect otherwise but there's no way they can be sure unless they're told. If necessary tell them we haven't been able to establish a link with any known crime yet, somebody is simply helping us with our enquiries. I think it will be a good idea to call on Hollingsworth, Davies and Matthews again to see if any of the three lads are known to them, we haven't broached the subject with any of them yet. Of course chances are that even if one or more of them is known to any of them they'll deny it anyway but if we watch them closely one of them may let something slip."

"You're still sure it's one of those three then, Guv?"

"Not really, but who else is there? I can't see where Matthews fits in, his only link is as a relative of the dead bus driver. The other two are more likely suspects but then only because they work on the buses and I'm sure it's an inside job, more so since talking to Jameson. The more we worry them the more certain I shall be one way or the other. The trouble is that motive is the big stumbling block, I still can't fathom what the motive could be for any of them, I'm certain it isn't just robbery, a couple of thousand pounds doesn't justify killing three people, possibly four if you include Jameson. Anyway, come on, let's get round there and see if they're in."

Their first call was at the Hollingsworth's in Berwick Road where the door was opened by a pretty young girl in school uniform.

"Hello," said the Inspector holding out his warrant card, "you must be Claire, we haven't met before, I'm Detective Inspector Harty and this is Detective Sergeant Tully, is your father at home?"

Before she could answer a voice from the passage behind her asked, "Who is it Claire?" and Stan Hollingsworth appeared at the door. "Oh, it's you again Inspector, getting to be quite a regular visitor, what can I do for you this time? You'd better come in."

As they entered the hall Freda Hollingsworth joined them and they all went into the living room.

"Just a couple more questions I'd like to ask you," said the Inspector, "it won't take long. Do you, or any of your family, know three young lads named Frank Prescott, Phil Jameson and Tim Priestley?"

At the mention of Tim Priestley's name Claire gave an involuntary gasp and they all looked at her. Her face reddened and she looked down at her feet.

"Is he the one?" asked Freda Hollingsworth taking hold of her daughter's arm, "Is that what you meant when you said it's too late? Oh Claire, that's awful."

Claire remained silent refusing to look at any of them.

"What's all this about?" asked Inspector Harty.

"Well, you'll have to know, I suppose," said Stan Hollingsworth, "Claire's pregnant but she won't tell us who the father is. Now, it seems, it might be this Priestley lad. He was the one found dead in the park wasn't he? Something to do with the robbery."

"When did you find out about Claire's condition?" asked the Inspector, ignoring Hollingsworth's question.

"Only yesterday morning, came like a bolt from the blue."

"Did you know Priestley?"

"No, I hadn't heard of him until I read about his death in the papers. If I'd known before I would probably have killed him myself, ruined Claire's life he has, she's only fourteen you know, had everything to look forward to before this!"

"It's hardly ruined her life, Stan." said Freda Hollingsworth, then turning to the Inspector, "Don't take too much notice of him, Inspector, he doesn't mean half the things he says. I've told him many times before that one day he'll get himself into trouble if he doesn't think before he speaks. He thinks the world of Claire and is very protective towards her. She will be having an abortion, by the way, but we want to keep that quiet."

"Did you know Tim Priestley, Mrs Hollingsworth?"

"No, I'm afraid not, as far as we knew Claire had no boyfriends. It all came as a big surprise to us. We both thought she was too busy with her school work and I suppose we shut our minds to the possibility, she's only fourteen after all. This Tim would have been too old for her anyway, seventeen, wasn't he? That's what it said in the papers. I think he must have taken advantage of her somehow. We've always been very open with Claire on the subject of sex and I'm sure she wouldn't have encouraged him in any way. I'll have to have a talk with her and see if I can get to the bottom of it."

"Do any of you know either of the other two boys?"

"What were their names again?" asked Stan Hollingsworth.

"Frank Prescott and Phil Jameson."

"Frank Prescott was that other one who was killed, burnt to death in a car on the waste ground, isn't that right?" asked Hollingsworth.

"Shot dead, then burnt," said the Inspector, "the newspapers tend to over dramatize things, but yes, you're right. Did you know him at all?"

"No, we didn't know him, nor the other one, Phil Jameson, you said, did we Freda?"

Freda Hollingsworth shook her head.

"Mind you I have seen Claire talking to a couple of lads after school but I don't know their names." said Hollingsworth. "I thought they looked a bit old for her perhaps I should have asked. I suppose this Phil Jameson you mentioned must have been the third one in the robbery then." said Hollingsworth, "Have you found him yet? Is he dead too? It didn't do them any good, did it? Serves them right for what happened to poor old Pete."

At this point Detective Inspector Harty felt he had achieved as much as he was going to so he and Sergeant Tully took their leave of the Hollingsworth's.

Outside, the Sergeant said, "Well, that was an interesting session, Guv, all sorts of things are creeping out of the woodwork now."

"Yes, Bob, and Hollingsworth certainly seems to have a motive for doing something to Priestley, at least, although killing him seems a bit drastic. If yesterday was the first they knew of Claire's condition Priestley was already dead anyway. Hollingsworth said that he didn't know Priestley but I'm not so sure. If you remember, the way I phrased the question when I asked if they knew any of the three lads any one of the names could have caused that reaction from Claire. She didn't mention Priestley, she didn't say anything. Her mother hinted that she knew but it was Hollingsworth who actually named him as the father. I can't see any link there with Prescott and Jameson though but I've still got an open mind. From what Jameson told us this morning it's more than likely that Priestley was known to Jimmy. I don't know if you noticed but we purposely avoided letting the papers know that Priestley was involved in the robbery, but Hollingsworth knew! Why would he want to kill Thompson, though? There's something still missing in this whole business. Let's get round to the Matthews' and see what they have to say."

Geoff Matthews was at home and answered the door to the two policemen. He wasn't at all happy to see them.

"This is getting beyond a joke, Inspector," he said, "I know you've got a job to do but why you keep hounding us I don't know. We've already told you all we know, which isn't much, what do you want this time?"

"We're hardly hounding you, sir," replied the Inspector, "we are just doing our job. I would have thought that you would have more reason than anyone to want to help find your cousin's killer. There are a couple of questions I would like to ask you and your wife, may we come in?"

"Mary!" called Matthews as they entered the house, "It's the police again, can you come down? They want to ask some more questions."

"Oh, and is your daughter in?" asked the Inspector.

"Kerry? What's she got to do with it?"

"Just routine, sir, nothing to worry about. She knows Claire Hollingsworth, doesn't she? Something has come up that we need a little more information on, if possible."

Kerry was called and, as she entered the room, her mother said, "Darling, this is Inspector Harty and

Sergeant Tully from the police. There's nothing to worry about, they just want to ask us a few questions about Claire."

"Why, what's she done?" asked Kerry.

"Nothing, as far as we know." said Inspector Harty, "How well do you know her?"

"They've been good friends for a long time now." said Mary Matthews.

"I would prefer Kerry to answer for herself if you don't mind, Mrs Matthews." said the Inspector, "Now, Kerry, how much can you tell me about Claire?"

"I don't know what you mean." replied Kerry, "We're in the same class at school and we've been friends for a long time. I don't know what else you want to know."

"Well, has she any boyfriends and, if so, do you know who they are?"

"She hasn't got any regular boyfriends. We both see some of the boys at school but most of them aren't worth bothering about, just a lot of kids, mostly."

"So you and Claire prefer older boys, perhaps?"

"Just what are you suggesting, Inspector?" demanded Geoff Matthews.

"Bear with me, sir, there is a good reason for this line of questioning. Well Kerry?"

"Oh, I expect you're talking about Tim. Now I know why you're here," Kerry replied, "Tim was a nice bloke, I'm sorry he's dead."

"What's this you're talking about?" cried Mary Matthews in alarm, "Who's this Tim and what do you mean you're sorry he's dead?"

"There's no need to get too alarmed, Mrs Matthews," said Inspector Harty, "haven't you read the papers? We're talking about Tim Priestley who was found dead in the park last Thursday. I can assure you your daughter has nothing to do with it, we're just trying to establish who knew him and what sort of lad he was."

"I don't like you asking my daughter these sort of questions," retorted Geoff Matthews, "I should have asked what you wanted before we brought her down here. She's only fourteen you know, what do you expect of her?"

"There's no harm in the questions, Mr Matthews," said Inspector Harty, "and I think you'll find that your daughter knows more than you give her credit for, she's a very bright girl you know."

"I don't mind answering the questions, dad," Kerry said, "We really didn't know Tim all that well really. He used to be waiting by the shops near the school most afternoons and walked part of the way home with us. He was very friendly and interesting to talk to."

"What have we always told you about talking to strangers." said Mary Matthews sharply, "especially men. Don't you ever do as you're told? How old was this Tim anyway?"

"He was seventeen," said the Inspector, "and I'm sure your daughter saw no harm in talking to him although I don't condone it myself. I must say that both your daughter and Claire Hollingsworth look a little older than their age even in school uniform. Perhaps Tim Priestley thought they were nearer his age. It would be only natural for him to try to chat them up."

"Claire and I were always together anyway, mum." said Kerry, "Neither of us were ever alone with him. I don't think he would have tried anything anyway, he wasn't that type."

"All boys are that type," grumbled Geoff Matthews, "no girl's safe with a seventeen year old boy."

"Are you sure Claire wasn't alone with him at some time or another?" asked the Inspector.

"Oh, you mean because she's pregnant!" exclaimed Kerry, "But that wasn't Tim....."

She realised that she had said something she hadn't intended to and shut up completely. At the mention of the word 'pregnant' Mary Matthews almost had a fit and Geoff Matthews looked ready to burst.

"If it wasn't Tim then who was it?" asked the Inspector.

Kerry refused to utter another word and ran from the room and upstairs to her bedroom where she closed the door behind her.

"Your superior's going to hear of this." said Geoff Matthews to Inspector Harty, "You come here without warning and start putting ideas into my daughter's head. We've tried to protect her from things like this and, in less than an hour, you've undone all our work."

"We're only doing our duty, sir," replied the Inspector, "They were questions that needed asking. We've got to get to the bottom of this case. As for putting ideas into your daughter's head I think it's about time you came down to earth and realised that , these days, children know an awful lot more than we ever did."

"I think you'd better go, Inspector, you've done enough damage."

"I haven't finished yet, sir. Did you or your wife know Tim Priestley?"

"I think it's quite obvious we didn't, don't you? Now goodbye!"

After they left the Matthews' the two policemen got into their car and made their way towards Harry Davies's bungalow.

"Matthews was a self-righteous twit!" exclaimed Sergeant Tully, "Seems to get less helpful each time we see him."

"He's just a bit over protective towards his daughter," said Inspector Harty, "a lot of fathers with only one child are like that especially if it's a girl, and she's a particularly pretty one. Can't say that I blame him really."

"You didn't ask them if they knew Prescott or Jameson, Guv, did you forget?"

"There didn't seem much point, Bob, we would probably have got the same reply we had from Hollingsworth and that was no help at all."

"What do you think the girl meant when she said it wasn't Priestley who made Claire Hollingsworth pregnant?"

"That's what I mean to find out, Bob. This case is developing in a way I didn't expect. Quite a few little titbits have come our way today."

They arrived at 55, Orchard Avenue and found that their luck was holding. Harry Davies was at home and was bent double over the engine compartment of a Ford Fiesta which had seen better days. He did not see the two policemen approaching and looked up with a start, bumping his head on the bonnet lid of the car, when the Inspector greeted him.

"Oh, it's you again Inspector." he said, rubbing the back of his head with a rather greasy hand. "I didn't hear you coming. I'm trying to get this old heap going again for a neighbour's son. The engine's just about had it, should be allowed to rest in peace I reckon, but his dad won't fork out for a replacement."

"Should it still be on the road?" asked Sergeant Tully.

"Oh, it's sound enough otherwise." replied Harry Davies, "It's only just passed its M.O.T. It's just that this engine has done a fair old mileage and is well worn, there's no room left for proper adjustment of the timing. Anyway, enough about that, what can I do for you? Is there any more news?"

"Is your wife at home?" asked Inspector Harty, "We would like to speak to you both together."

"Yes, she's here." said Davies, "Probably in the kitchen. Come this way."

He took them down the side of the bungalow and round to the back door. The Inspector could not resist another look in the garage as they walked past it and marvelled once again at the equipment it contained.

"Sylvie, love," called Davies as they entered the door, "are you there? The police are here again and want to speak to us both."

Sylvia Davies was standing by the kitchen sink and greeted them. "I've just put the kettle on," she said, "would you like a cup of tea?"

"No thank you," replied the Inspector, "we won't be here long. There are just a couple of questions we would like to ask you both."

"Right, fire away." said Davies, "We shall try to help you in any way we can."

"Last time we were here it was mentioned that youngsters used to call to try to get work on your cars." said the Inspector, "I wonder if, by any chance, the name Frank Prescott means anything to you? We know that he was keen on cars and, until recently, had a job as motor mechanic with a local garage."

"Frank Prescott was that lad who was found dead on the old railway sidings, wasn't he?" replied Davies, "An awful business that was, made me shudder when I read about it in the paper. No, Inspector, I hadn't heard the name before that. There was a picture of him in the paper I remember. No, he wasn't one of the lads who came round here. Sorry, can't help you there."

"What about you, Mrs Davies?" asked the Inspector.

Sylvia Davies just shook her head.

"O.K." said Inspector Harty, "Does the name Philip Jameson mean anything?"

Both Harry and Sylvia Davies slowly shook their heads. "No," said Harry, "never heard of that one."

"How about Tim Priestley?"

"Are they the three young thugs involved in the bus robbery?" asked Davies, "So you know who they are then. What about the ring leader, the bastard who shot poor old Pete, have you got him yet?"

"Please answer my question, Mr Davies. Do you know Tim Priestley?"

"He was the one found dead in the park, wasn't he?" asked Sylvia Davies before Harry could reply, "A boy named Tim used to come round here quite a lot, I didn't know his surname, but the picture in the paper looked a lot like him. It wasn't a very good picture though, it was blurred and was taken a long time ago when he was a lot younger but I'm sure it was him. I said so to you, didn't I Harry?"

"That wasn't the same Tim!" exclaimed Harry, rather too quickly, "That newspaper picture didn't look at all like the lad who used to come here, I told you so, Sylvie, when you pointed it out to me. You never have been very good at recognising faces."

Sylvia Davies said nothing more but hung her head in embarrassment at having said anything at all.

"Well, thank you both for your help." said the Inspector, "That will be all for now."

Back in their car the Inspector said to Sergeant Tully, "So Davies knew Tim Priestley then. Despite his denial I'm certain of it and it was obvious that he didn't want us to know. I'll bet he's cursing his wife for letting that slip. Things are looking very black for him. Everything points to him being our man but we have absolutely nothing concrete on which to base a charge. It all hinges on

Jameson's identification. Thank goodness he was found in time, without him it would all be pretty hopeless."

Five minutes after they had returned to West Town police station Detective Constable Robson entered Inspector Harty's office and said, "We have managed to break the password on Thompson's computer system at last, Guv. He certainly didn't want anyone to get into that in a hurry, we had half a dozen experts working on it in the end, and now we know why he had made it so difficult."

"What could be so important on a home computer system to need such tight security?" asked the Inspector.

"It seems that Thompson was part of a paedophile ring," replied Robson, "probably the ringleader in fact. The stuff he's got on that computer disk is a real eye opener. There's a whole database of contacts from all over the country and in most of Europe too. One or two of the names we've found are going to cause quite a stir. People you just wouldn't believe could be involved in anything like that."

"People like that disgust me, whoever they are!" exclaimed Detective Inspector Harty, "They deserve everything they get when caught, and more. To my mind no punishment is hard enough. Children should be allowed to live their short lives completely free of anything to do with sex and drugs, there's time enough for that when they grow up and can please themselves what they get up to."

"Well, Bob," he continued, this time to Sergeant Tully, "we knew from what we already had that Thompson wasn't interested in women but liked to watch hard porn videos, that was, perhaps, a bit unnatural but nevertheless understandable. Now this latest revelation, it puts a whole new complexion on the case. I wonder if anyone else round here, apart from those on his computer list, knew of his sexual preferences."

"Everybody we've spoken to have said what a nice bloke he was," said Sergeant Tully, "a little weird but harmless is the worst we've heard of him. Surely if anybody knew what he was up to they would have said something. I can't imagine any normal person, especially with a family, not only keeping quiet about it but praising him."

"You're probably right, Bob, but people do strange and unexpected things, don't forget. I think I'll have another run through the statements we've had so far before I go home tonight, there might be something there that makes more sense now that this has come to light. There's no need for you to hang around any longer I'll see you in the morning."

Chapter eighteen

Detective Inspector Harty was up and about bright and early the following morning. Without disturbing his wife he prepared himself a quick and easy breakfast of tea and toast and scanned through the previous day's newspaper while he ate it. It was too early for this morning's delivery but while he was involved in a case like this one his mind was too full of his own problems to be bothered too much with anything the newspaper might offer. When he had finished he quietly washed up the crockery he had used and crept upstairs to peep round the bedroom door. Satisfied that his wife was not yet awake he crept back downstairs, put on his hat and coat and made his way to his car and West Town police station.

The weather was calm with no hint of a breeze and with a bright early morning sun rising in a cloudless blue sky. It showed promise of a perfect spring day to match his own optimism about the outcome of the case which was, he was sure, nearing a conclusion. He knew better than to count his chickens, so to speak, he had seen too many cases over the years where an arrest had seemed imminent only to be foiled by something unforeseen or because the evidence gathered had not proved strong enough. He knew only too well that the bulk of the evidence they had so far was circumstantial and relied heavily on the truthfulness and accuracy of the story told by Phil Jameson. He also knew that only Jameson, and nobody else, could positively identify the man, Jimmy, they were after. Finding Jameson alive had been their biggest break. If Jimmy had found him first there was no doubt at all that he would now be just another body in the mortuary along with Prescott and Priestley. Jimmy was an extremely dangerous man who had to be caught sooner rather than later. With Jameson's help it would hopefully be soon, without it it would very probably be much later, if at all.

Today was Wednesday, just over a week since the robbery, the day of bus driver Pete Thompson's funeral with all the pomp that the bus company could afford. It was also the day of Frank Prescott's funeral but that was to be a small private family affair in another part of town well away from the cemetery where the others would be. It would probably be attended by only his mother and two sisters and perhaps a couple of close friends. He had, after all, died a criminal in the eyes of the community.

Inspector Harty thought about Jameson's fondness for Prescott and of how he had explained Prescott's involvement in the robbery. He then thought of the information they had gathered so far about Thompson, particularly about his involvement with young children of which there was no doubt, and considered that here was a criminal far in excess of anything that young Prescott might be but it was not common knowledge, none of the information they had gathered had yet been released to the public. As far as the world at large was concerned Thompson was an innocent victim of a ruthless killer while simply doing his job. This line of thought led Inspector Harty to wonder whether Thompson's perversion had any bearing on the case. Was Jimmy aware of Thompson's background? Did it have any connection with the murder? If so why the robbery and why involve the three young lads? There were still a host of questions to be answered but the Inspector felt sure that, once Jimmy was captured, the pieces would fall into place.

Thinking back to the funeral the Inspector wondered if the bus company would have been so lavish with the arrangements if they had been aware of Thompson's perversions. Probably not. They knew him only as a long serving and reliable employee who had bravely tried to thwart a robbery and were aiming to use the occasion to gain a bit of public support. Good public relations were important to them after all. If Thompson's background was public knowledge then laying on a show like the one planned would have exactly the opposite effect.

The Inspector looked at the papers in front of him and noticed, for the first time and with some annoyance, that both funerals were due to take place at about the same time. Thompson's was timed for eleven o'clock with the cortege leaving the bus depot at twenty past ten while Prescott's was to take place at ten forty-five. Why hadn't he, or anybody else, spotted that earlier? It was too late to do anything about it now. The arrangements by the bus company were too complex to change at short notice and it would be totally unfair and hard hearted to expect Prescott's family to change their preparations today. The problem was that if Jimmy was to attend the funeral of his victim which one would be the most likely? Probably Thompson's, especially if, as Inspector Harty now suspected, he had killed Thompson because of his perversions. On the other hand he may be feeling remorseful about the way he had got rid of Prescott and could attend his funeral as a way of trying to make some amends. The big argument against that, however, was that at Thompson's funeral he could lose himself in the crowd while at Prescott's he would surely stand out like a sore thumb. If Jimmy worked for the bus company, as the Inspector also suspected, he would not have much choice. He would have to attend Thompson's funeral or give himself away.

Jameson had already requested to be present at his friend's funeral and, while no promises had been made,

Inspector Harty was a man of compassion and was very reluctant to deny his request. The two lads had, after all, been very close for a long time and it was only natural that Jameson would want to say his last farewells. His story of the robbery and that he and Prescott had been convinced that it was all part of some rag day prank had a very strong ring of truth about it. They both came across as basically honest lads who had been hoodwinked and, while it wasn't his place to judge, the Inspector felt that Jameson should be allowed to attend his friend's funeral. It was out of the question that he could attend both, the cemeteries were too far apart for that to be possible. Suddenly, Inspector Harty felt rather less optimistic, the ready made opportunity for Jameson to point the finger at Jimmy was slipping away.

Detective Sergeant Tully arrived at the police station just before eight o'clock and went directly to Inspector Harty's office.

"Good morning, Guv," he said, "you're an early bird today, couldn't you sleep, or has something happened to bring you in?"

"Neither Bob," the Inspector replied, "I've been thinking of what Robson told us yesterday about Thompson's sexual preferences. You know, it puts a completely different aspect on the case. I'm wondering if Jimmy was aware of it and if that was the reason Thompson was killed."

"I see what you mean, Guv. The robbery could just have been a blind to put us off the trail. We've been assuming that the bus driver recognised Jimmy and that was the reason he was killed. The thing that puzzles me though is that if the main intention was to kill Thompson then why not do it quietly somewhere else? Why go to the lengths to stage such an elaborate hold-up and why involve and murder three young lads? All right, I know he didn't murder Jameson but we are both certain the intention was there, probably still is. There would have been much less chance of our catching Jimmy if he had just bumped off the bus driver in a dark alley or somewhere like that. As it is we're pulling out all the stops to catch him and, if I know you, Guv, catch him we certainly will."

"Perhaps Jimmy had so much hatred for Thompson that he wanted to do it as publicly as possible, Bob, so that the truth was sure to come out." said the Inspector, "Who knows, perhaps he wants to be caught and punished for the killing, stranger things have happened. It could be that he murdered Prescott and Priestley to make absolutely sure of being caught, and is still looking for Jameson to the same end. The only thing against that argument is that he is covering his tracks so well. In my experience people who want to get caught leave clues all over the place. Our man has left nothing whatsoever to lead us to him. The man can't be right in the head though to kill as ruthlessly as he has, intense hatred can do that. We both know that when a man has killed once it becomes much easier for him to do it again and, in some cases, it eventually becomes an obsession. That's how serial killers are born"

"You've had a bee in your bonnet all along about Hollingsworth and Matthews, Guv." said Sergeant Tully, " Has it occurred to you that Thompson used to take both their daughters out for trips occasionally? Those two girls would be in the right age group for the likes of him, wouldn't they? Could it be that one of the fathers is the killer after all?"

"Yes, it has occurred to me, Bob, and, what's more, I keep recalling young Kerry Matthews' outburst just before we left there yesterday. Do you remember? When I mentioned Claire Hollingsworth she said ,'you mean because she's pregnant, but that wasn't Tim'. It didn't mean a lot at the time but since Robson's revelations about Thompson it makes me wonder if there isn't something in it. Of course it could just mean that somebody totally unrelated to the case was the father."

"It would certainly give Hollingsworth one hell of a motive if Thompson had been messing about with his daughter and made her pregnant, Guv. So you think it was him then?"

"I didn't say that, Bob. You must bear in mind that according to the Hollingsworth's they had no idea that Claire was pregnant until the other day and we have no reason to think otherwise. If that was so then at the time of the robbery that motive didn't exist. Another thing, on almost every occasion we've spoken to Hollingsworth he's said what a nice guy Thompson was and there was nothing in his tone of voice, or face expressions either, to make us disbelieve that. He obviously dotes on his daughter and could probably kill if he thought anything like that was happening to her but I don't somehow think he could talk of Thompson the way he did without giving something away of his true feelings. Of course I could be wrong, actors do it all the time, but that's not quite the same."

"Yes, Guv, of course you're right." replied the Sergeant, "I'm jumping to conclusions again. What do you think about Matthews though?"

"Well, he hasn't been the most helpful of people and I don't think he had a lot of time for Thompson, even though he was his cousin, he's made that quite clear. However, again there's been no hint from him, or his wife, that Thompson was anything other than he seemed to be and they both gave the impression that they were quite happy for Thompson to associate with their daughter Kerry. It was obvious that they certainly didn't know

172

about Claire's pregnancy until their daughter blurted it out yesterday. No, Bob, there's still nothing to link either Matthews or Hollingsworth to the robbery, but at the same time I'm not writing either of them off yet. There's still Davies to consider too. Of the three he is still, to my mind, the most likely suspect. Everything, although circumstantial, points to him except the sexual aspect. Paedophiles like Thompson, though, don't stop at little girls for their fun and games and Davies could be more fond and protective towards the lads who have wanted to work with him than he cares to admit. But that line of thought doesn't stand up when you consider the killing of Prescott and Priestley. It's hardly the thing somebody who is fond of youngsters would do. No, I'm afraid we keep going round in circles."

"We'll have to be getting off to the funeral soon." interrupted Detective Sergeant Tully looking at the clock on the wall, "I'll go and get Jameson from the cells, I assume we're taking him with us? Perhaps at last we shall know just who Jimmy is. He's almost certain to be there."

"Oh yes, Bob, the funeral. Did you know that Prescott's funeral is also taking place this morning, at practically the same time as Thompson's? That's just a small detail that we all overlooked. Jameson, naturally, wants to attend his friend's funeral and I really think he should. After all he did witness Prescott's death and it was a particularly nasty end to a young life. Yes, I know," the Inspector continued anticipating the Sergeant's objection, "but we really don't have much choice. We are not unfeeling ogres whatever people may think. We may still be lucky, Jimmy is just as likely to be there as at Thompson's."

"Not if it really is Hollingsworth, Davies or Matthews," retorted the Sergeant, "they've all got to be either at Thompson's funeral or at work at the bus depot."

173

"We shall keep a close eye on them, Bob, don't worry. Of course it's a pity it's worked out like this, I've no doubt that Jameson could have done us proud if there was just the one funeral but, never mind, it can't be helped the damage is done. I would like you to take Jameson to Prescott's funeral, if you don't mind. Just watch him closely. D.C. Robson and W.P.C. Wright can come with me to the main do."

Detective Inspector Harty instructed D.C. Robson to drive the car straight to the cemetery where Thompson was to be buried. He had no intention of getting involved with the show which was being arranged to get the body there and which would, by now, be already well under way. He was not to be there, after all, as a mourner but simply as an onlooker to see if anything could be spotted to help him with the case. That would certainly be harder without Jameson and he rather doubted the wisdom of attending at all but something may come to light.

They had been waiting for almost ten minutes when the cortege started to enter the cemetery gates. Leading the procession were two professional undertakers dressed in black frock coats and top hats, walking with heads slightly bowed and with their hands clasped in front of them. Then came the hearse carrying the highly polished oak coffin with gleaming brass fittings and laden with wreaths of flowers from the Matthews and Hollingsworth families and from the bus company. Following this was a sleek, black limousine containing the principal mourners, Thompson's only family, Geoff and Mary Matthews and their daughter, Kerry. A second limousine carried Freda Hollingsworth and her daughter, Claire, the manager of the bus depot and the managing director of the bus company. After this there were two double decker buses, specially cleaned inside and out for the occasion, displaying details for route 37 on the destination boards, the route on which the murder and robbery took place and which was Thompson's usual route. Driving the first bus, as a tribute to Thompson, was Stan Hollingsworth. The upper decks of both buses were unoccupied while the lower decks carried the bus and maintenance crews who had worked with Thompson over the years. They also carried numerous colourful wreaths and sprays of flowers donated by workmates and others in memory of the dead driver.

As the cortege came to a halt outside the chapel doors, Stan Hollingsworth climbed down from the cab of his bus and, together with five other men from the same bus, all smartly dressed in brand new bus company uniforms, moved to the rear of the hearse to act as pall bearers and carried the coffin into the chapel.

Detective Inspector Harty, with D.C. Robson and W.P.C. Wright, stood at a discreet distance while they watched the coffin carried into the chapel followed by the people from the cars and buses. They carefully scanned the faces of the crowd as it entered the chapel but there was nothing helpful to see. Without Jameson it was hopeless. They waited outside for the funeral service to finish and for the burial ceremony to begin. So far they had seen nothing out of the ordinary and nobody who should not have been there. They constantly gazed around the cemetery to see if Jimmy could be waiting there as an unobtrusive observer but the only other people in sight were two women tending a grave on the other side of the roadway.

After thirty minutes or so had passed the chapel doors opened and the coffin was placed in the hearse to be carried to a prepared grave some distance inside the cemetery. The Matthews family re-entered their limousine, which trailed the hearse at walking pace, while the rest of the mourners followed on foot. The police kept their distance, not wanting to interfere in any way with the proceedings, while continuing to keep a watchful eye for anything unusual.

"I thought it was to be a cremation." remarked the Inspector, "The manager at the depot must have persuaded Matthews to have a burial after all, it's what the bus company wanted. It's amazing what a little bit of money can do, I'm assuming bribery was involved!"

The burial was almost over, the coffin had been lowered into the grave and the priest was saying the last words of the burial service, when the Inspector's two way radio suddenly came to life. In the quietness of the surroundings the radio seemed particularly loud and every word could be clearly heard by everyone there. All heads turned to look at the Inspector, some with annoyance, as the unmistakeable voice of Detective Sergeant Tully came over the air.

"I'm very sorry, Guv," he was saying, "I don't know how it happened but Jameson has given us the slip. One moment he was standing at my side by Frank Prescott's grave. I turned my head briefly and, when I looked back, he wasn't there. There's no sign of him here at the cemetery. It's the last thing I expected, he had been so co-operative up to then. It's a stupid thing for him to do."

Inspector Harty turned his back on the mourners at the grave side, most of whom, now that the burial service was finished, were talking among themselves and casting furtive glances in the Inspector's direction.

"I'll see you back at the station," he said into his radio, "there's nothing more we can do here now. With Jameson on the loose it's imperative we find him before Jimmy does."

To himself he thought 'If Jimmy is here he now knows for certain that Jameson is around and roughly where he might be.'

He beckoned D.C. Robson and W.P.C. Wright to follow him to the car. They left the cemetery and drove quickly back to West Town.

Chapter nineteen

Back at Detective Inspector Harty's office in West Town police station the Inspector and Sergeant Tully got together to discuss the latest development.

"Well, Bob," said Inspector Harty, "everybody who was at Thompson's funeral now knows that Phil Jameson is on the loose and is definitely in the local area. If Jimmy was at that funeral, as I'm pretty sure he was, he must really have thought it was his lucky day when your message came through. I haven't the slightest doubt that he will be out and about looking for Jameson at the earliest opportunity. I only hope Jameson knows what he's got to do and doesn't take too many chances."

"It was a very clever idea of yours, Guv, to have him run off like that." replied the Sergeant, "The timing was brilliant. Personally, I'm convinced that Jimmy was at Thompson's funeral, he certainly wasn't at Prescott's. As we expected, apart from the vicar, Jameson and myself, the only other people there were Prescott's mother and his two young sisters and Mrs Parkin, Jameson's aunt. That churchyard was a very small place compared to the cemetery where you were and there is no way anybody else could have been there without being seen. Mrs Prescott was very pleased to see Phil Jameson there, by the way. It obviously went some way to brightening up a very gloomy day for her, and the relief on Mrs Parkin's face was clear to see. I know now you did the right thing in letting him go to that funeral. I must admit that when you told me Jameson was to attend Prescott's funeral I thought you were throwing away our only chance of getting Jimmy but now, hopefully, we should be able to catch him red handed."

"It was the only way I could see of making the best of a bad job but we've got Jameson to thank for agreeing to my plan, Bob. It's extremely dangerous for him you know. I hope you've got him well covered, we'll both be for the high jump if things go wrong now and Jimmy does manage to get to him after all. That's something we've got to prevent at all costs."

"Don't worry, there shouldn't be any trouble Guv." replied the Sergeant, "Jameson is in safe hands. I've got three of our best men tailing him at all times. They are all very reliable and certainly won't let him out of their sight. They won't be obvious enough to scare Jimmy off either. The moment Jimmy makes his move they'll be there to make the arrest. They are in constant radio contact with each other and, just to be on the safe side, Jameson has been fitted with an electronic tracker so that, if they do happen to lose sight of him, they'll still know he's there. We've just got to hope that Jimmy doesn't take too long to make his move. The longer this type of surveillance lasts the more likely a slip up of some kind could occur."

"I don't think we would be able to stand a long wait with a thing like this." said the Inspector, "I'm convinced Jimmy will try something this afternoon. The way his mind works I don't think he will be able to resist doing something at the earliest opportunity. If Jameson follows the instructions I gave him this morning he shouldn't be too hard to find and it shouldn't be obvious to anyone that he's acting as bait. If I'm right Jimmy will be too obsessed with what he intends to do to notice too much whether it's a set up or not anyway."

"What do you intend to do if nothing does happen this afternoon, Guv? Jameson can't wander around the streets for ever and we've got to justify what we're doing to the Chief."

"I've decided to give it twenty four hours at most, Bob. If nothing has happened by this time tomorrow we'll call it a day and think up some other plan. There's a limit to the amount of time we can commit this sort of manpower to the case anyway. I don't think there will be any problem though, I've got a gut feeling about this and am sure Jimmy will be behind bars by tonight. I managed to have a few words with Jameson's aunt, Mrs Parkin, by the way, and made some arrangements with her. If he is still out by eleven tonight he's been told to go to her house for bed, she's very happy to have him there, and he can carry on again in the morning. We can arrange to cover the house overnight in case Jimmy gets it into his head to try something there. As you said, Mrs Parkin was very relieved that we had her nephew, she was sure he had gone the same way as Prescott and Priestley. It's nice when you can give someone some good news for a change. Incidentally, both she and Mrs Prescott were put in the picture about Jameson's apparent escape from the crematorium, I didn't see the point in causing them more worry than is necessary."

"I'll have to let my men know about tonight's arrangements," said Sergeant Tully, "I can get a couple of volunteers to watch the house overnight. The other three may as well get some sleep so that they are fresh for tomorrow."

As Phil Jameson ran through the church gates he couldn't help wondering what he had let himself in for this time. It had taken Detective Inspector Harty some time to persuade him to fake an escape from the churchyard that morning but, in the end, the fact that he would be doing something positive to catch Frankie's killer had won him over. He just hoped that it wouldn't take too long. He had already experienced more than a week on the run and it was something he didn't really want to do again. All right, it was different this time, he wasn't really on the run, people who cared were looking after him, he was to try to get Jimmy to find him. His head was in a bit of a spin. He was finding it difficult to come to terms with his new role. The police, this time, were following him wherever he went, at least he hoped they were, he couldn't see them anywhere, but there was no reason to think that the Inspector would not keep his word. He would just have to keep a wary eye open for Jimmy. He was the bait to catch the fish and he didn't want to end up dead. Only a few hours earlier, before he had been found at the rubbish tip, he had reached the stage where he really couldn't have cared less whether Jimmy found him or not, but now he definitely wanted to stay alive and wished that this was all over. He accepted that he would probably go to prison for his part in the robbery but then he deserved that for being so stupid. If only he hadn't involved Frankie. That thought went through his mind for the umpteenth time.

He had found that he rather liked Inspector Harty. The Inspector came across as a genuine and compassionate man. Not at all like the kind of policeman he had come to expect. He knew instinctively that the Inspector would do all he could to make sure no harm came to him. During the long interview at the police station the Inspector had seemed like a sort of father figure coaxing information from him and making him feel that he could tell everything as it had happened and that he had no reason to lie. He couldn't help wishing his own father had been like that, perhaps he wouldn't be in this predicament now if things had been different at home. He couldn't understand why his mother and father disliked him so much although it was mostly his father who had a go at him. His mother was a rather meek little woman who did everything his father demanded.

Frankie had been the only one to stand by him and give him the help he had needed although Aunt Audrey had certainly been more than a mother to him than his own mum had. However, she had her own family to think of and, as he grew older, he had been reluctant to take too much advantage of her generosity. Frankie had let him share the flat even though it was obvious that he wouldn't be able to pay his way. Frankie had been the best friend anybody could possibly have and had been repaid in the worst possible way! Why couldn't he, Jameson, have been driving that car instead? Perhaps then Frankie would still be alive instead of him. That would have been much more fair, but he knew that could not have happened because he was nowhere near as good a driver as Frankie had been. He would never be able to forget what had happened to Frankie and would never be able to forgive himself for getting involved with Jimmy. As the name Jimmy went through his mind, Phil Jameson came out of his reverie and remembered what he was supposed to be doing. He took stock of his bearings and looked around to see if he could spot the policemen who were trailing him. Either they were very good at their job or his powers of observation were much worse than he thought they were. There was hardly anybody else about that he could see, a woman with a shopping basket walking along the other side of the road and a young man further down the road crouching down looking at his bike as if he was having trouble with the chain. The thought went through his mind that perhaps Detective Sergeant Tully hadn't yet detailed anyone to follow him and a shiver of fear crept up his spine. The Sergeant was a different kettle of fish altogether to the Inspector, nowhere near as patient and friendly as the Inspector had been. But Jameson pushed those thoughts out of his head, after all, the police were just as anxious to catch Jimmy as he was to be free from the danger, they must be out there somewhere watching his every move. If they weren't then it would certainly be 'goodbye Phil Jameson', he hadn't a hope of defending himself against a madman like Jimmy.

He found that he was approaching the gates to the park, close to the spot where Tim Priestley had been murdered and an involuntary shudder went through his body. Would Jimmy be mad enough to do it again in the same place? What were the chances of meeting Jimmy again anyway? Pretty slim, he thought, just by wandering about the streets, unless of course Jimmy knew within reason where he might be. Perhaps the police might have a good idea who Jimmy is and somehow might have given him some clues in order to trap him. The Inspector had been quite specific on the sort of route to take, but he had also given the impression, very strongly, that he had no idea who Jimmy really was.

Phil Jameson decided to enter the park and made his way towards the lake where he had spent many happy hours during his school days. Thinking back he realised that it must have been almost four years now since he was here last but, already, it seemed an eternity. So much had happened and so much had gone wrong since he had left school, if only he could put the clock back!

As he approached the lake he could see the rowing boats lined up at the water's edge as if eagerly waiting for customers. It was a nice, sunny afternoon but there weren't many people about. The kids were still all at school, it would be a couple of hours yet before they would be out and laughing and shouting their way through the park. There were a couple of boats out on the lake, courting couples probably, taking advantage of the solitude offered in a small rowing boat in the centre of a sizeable lake. He found the thought very attractive and decided to hire a boat and spend a half-hour or so out there himself. He wondered what his police followers would make of it and whether they would follow suit but, at the moment, he didn't care too much, he wanted some time to himself to get his thoughts together and work out what he would do if Jimmy was to find him. The Inspector had told him not to take chances and to stay where the policemen could easily get to him but he found it hard to resist the lure of the water.

He paid his money at the booth and stepped into the boat offered to him. As he rowed away from the edge of the lake he looked both ways along the footpath to see if he could spot his trackers. Again there was nothing obvious and he marvelled at their expertise. They must be there somewhere but nobody else was making towards the boats and the only people he could see were a couple sitting together on a bench at the lake side and they seemed to be too interested in each other to have any interest in him.

Back at West Town police station Detective Inspector Harty and Detective Sergeant Tully were sitting together in the Inspector's office drinking coffee.

"I hate this waiting and sitting around doing nothing." said the Sergeant, "I wish we were out there with Jameson and on the spot when Jimmy turns up."

"I know only too well how you feel, Bob," returned the Inspector, "I hate it too but Jimmy undoubtedly knows both of us by sight and would spot us a mile off. That would do us no good at all, he would know it's a trap and would steer well clear of Jameson. The only way we can net him is for him to make a positive attempt on Jameson's life and he will only do that if he thinks the coast is clear. Hopefully we won't have to wait too long for him to react but I don't really expect anything to happen for a couple of hours yet. If he was at Thompson's funeral and heard your message over the radio he would be anxious to get things moving but couldn't afford to give himself away by moving too soon. He will have to spend some time at the wake to avoid looking disrespectful but I'll bet he's on edge. Robson's there in case anything unexpected happens and he's had instructions not to follow if anyone leaves early but to let us know immediately over the radio. Meanwhile we can't afford to take any chances at all while Jameson's out and about so we'll have to be patient and wait here until some news, one way or the other, comes through."

"You're right of course, Guv, but time drags so at times like this. It's the one part of police work I don't like but, I must admit, the rest of the job more than makes up for it."

At two o'clock a message came through from Robson.

"Everything's coming to an end here, Guv," he reported, "they are all leaving and nothing out of the ordinary has happened. Nobody left early, they've all been standing around eating and talking. I don't think any of them can know about Thompson's paedophile connections. It couldn't have gone off so quietly if they did."

"OK Frank," said Inspector Harty, "you make your way back here. Don't do anything to make any of them suspicious, things are going quite well so far."

Fifteen minutes later another call came through, this time from one of Jameson's three followers.

"Jameson's in a row-boat on the lake, Guv, we can watch him clearly from here. There's nowhere he can go on the other side there's a six foot fence right along the edge. It would be pointless for us to do the same, we wouldn't be able to get to him quickly enough if we did.

We've just spotted Hollingsworth and Davies coming across the park together, they are using the footpath that goes past the lake. There's no way of knowing whether they've seen Jameson yet but I should think he's too far away to be recognised. Wait, Davies has turned off and is walking away from the lake but Hollingsworth is still coming this way."

The Inspector looked at Sergeant Tully.

"What are they doing there?" he asked, "And why are they together? Davies is probably on his way home but Hollingsworth lives in the opposite direction. Is he our man after all?"

To the policeman at the park he said "Don't make any move unless Hollingsworth does. Keep in touch and tell us everything that happens. Whatever you do keep a close eye on Jameson. If Hollingsworth is Jimmy and Jameson spots him there's no telling what he'll do. It's a pity he's in that boat. I don't want everything fouled up at this stage."

To Sergeant Tully he said, "Nothing goes as expected, does it Bob? Why did the two of them have to turn up? I would like to find out for sure where Davies is going but we can't take anyone away from Jameson now."

Chapter twenty

The wake for the dead bus driver, Pete Thompson, was held at the Matthews' house and almost everybody who had been at the funeral and did not have to return immediately to work had collected there. Mary Matthews was not very happy to have so many people treading through her immaculate rooms, particularly as she had never been very fond of her husband's cousin, but she put a brave face on it all. What caused her most consternation, however, was that Stan Hollingsworth had brought most of them from the funeral in one of the buses used for the cortege and the yellow monstrosity was parked in the road outside the house. What would the neighbours think?

The second bus had been driven back to the depot by Harry Davies as soon as the funeral was over and he had taken back with him all those employees who were still on duty but allowed to attend the funeral.

The managing director of the bus company, together with the depot manager, stayed just long enough at the Matthews' house for one quick drink and to give Geoff and Mary Matthews their final condolences then took their leave and made their own way back to the depot.

Stan Hollingsworth ate a couple of sandwiches, more out of social grace than necessity, then finished his drink and put the glass down on the living room table. He went across to his wife, Freda, who was talking with a group of other busmen's wives.

"I've got to take the bus back to the depot, love," he said, "I expect the neighbours will be glad to see the back of it. By the look Mary keeps giving me I don't think she'll be sorry to see it go either. Will you be all right to make your own way home? There's no need to hurry it's a couple of hours yet before I'm on duty so, when I've got rid of the bus, I'll pop back home and get changed and put my feet up for a while."

Freda nodded and smiled at him, then said mechanically, "mind how you go." and returned to continue to gossip with the other women.

Before he left, Stan looked around for Geoff Matthews and when he found him said, "Well, Geoff, we certainly gave Pete a good send-off, didn't we? You and Mary have done him proud here too. Pity he wasn't here to see it, eh? I shall miss him, he's been a good mate to me. I expect you and Mary will miss him too and our two girls will miss their outings, won't they? I'm off now, got to take the bus back to the depot. Thanks for all you've done. I expect we shall see each other around from time to time."

Geoff Matthews simply replied "OK." and then, after a moment's thought, said "Wait a moment Stan, is it right what I hear, that your Claire's pregnant?"

"'Fraid so but it's no use crying over spilt milk, is it? Anyway, it's early days yet and, if I have my way, she'll probably have an abortion, don't want her ruining her young life with a kid before she's had a chance to enjoy herself."

"Have you any idea who the father is?"

"Not really, Claire's not saying much, but, reading between the lines so to speak, it seems it might have been that Priestley lad, the one who was killed in the park last week. Apparently she had been seeing him."

"That seems to fit in with something Kerry said," said Matthews, "but Priestley was quite a bit older than her wasn't he? Girls are a constant worry, aren't they, but you can't keep behind them twenty four hours a day. Something like that happening to our Kerry is always on my mind. I don't know what I would do if it did. I must say you seem to be taking it well enough."

"I don't know about that," replied Hollingsworth, "it knocked me sideways when I found out. I'm still stewing about it inside but Freda has helped me to see sense. I'll tell you this, if that Tim Priestley was still alive he would have some answering to do. Anyway I must be off. See you!"

After leaving the bus at the depot he decided to leave his car there too and walk home. It was a nice afternoon and he could do with a bit of fresh air to clear his head. He hated funerals, especially burials, they were so depressing, and trying to make small talk afterwards had given him a head ache.

As he walked towards the depot entrance he met Harry Davies, also leaving on foot.

"Hello Harry," he said, "where's your car? It's unusual to see you walking. Where are you off to?"

"I'm on my way home, Stan." Davies replied, "I didn't know what was happening after the funeral so Sylvie dropped me off this morning, she needed the van anyway."

"I'll walk along with you if you don't mind." said Hollingsworth, "It's a bit out of my way but you go through the park to your place, don't you? I fancy a walk through the park on an afternoon like this."

Davies grunted in reluctant assent and they made their way together towards the park gates.

As they walked along a park footpath that led to the boating lake Davies indicated another path branching to the right and said, "I'll leave you here, Stan. It's quicker for me to get home that way. It's been nice walking with you, perhaps we can do it again one day."

"Of course, why not." replied Hollingsworth, "I'll see you at the depot sometime. Goodbye."

As Hollingsworth continued his walk towards the lake he was thinking how pleasant it was. Very quiet with hardly anybody about and only a couple of boats out on the lake. He was thinking that it had been a very long time since he had been on the lake himself, he and Freda used to enjoy it before they married. Then he noticed that one of the boats contained only one young man and wondered what he was doing out there on his own. It was usual to see a boy and a girl in the boat together. Perhaps this young man was getting in a bit of practice before taking his girl out. He was on his way back to the landing stage and had his back to Hollingsworth, either his time was up or he'd had enough. The young man looked over his shoulder to see how much farther he had to go and Hollingsworth gave a start as he caught a glimpse of his face. Hollingsworth walked over to where the empty boats were lined up and stood there to wait until the young man had moored.

At West Town police station another message came over the radio. "Hollingsworth is waiting for Jameson to come in, Guv. He's obviously recognised him. I don't think Jameson has seen him yet he's still making straight for the berth. Hollingsworth can't possibly do anything here, it's too open. What do you want us to do?"

"Don't do anything unless Hollingsworth makes a move against Jameson physically," replied the Inspector, "but be ready to move very quickly if he does. Nothing must happen to Jameson but until we've got something positive to go on there's nothing we can do. If Jameson shows any sign of agitation as Hollingsworth approaches him then that's good enough, go in quickly. Otherwise do nothing to let him know you're there."

"Jameson is getting out of the boat now, Guv, and Hollingsworth is walking up to him. Jameson has just seen him but has shown no sign of recognition."

Stan Hollingsworth watched as the rowing boat approached the edge of the lake and while the attendant tied up the boat and held it steady as Jameson stepped out. He then walked up to Jameson.

"Hello son," he said, "I know you, don't I? Not your name but I've seen you with my daughter a couple of times, more than just friendly towards each other I'd say."

"I don't think so," replied Jameson, "I don't know who you are and I don't know which girl is your daughter, I know quite a few girls but I'm not going steady with anyone."

"Just how many have you got for crying out loud? Claire, I'm talking about, Claire Hollingsworth., you do know she's only fourteen, don't you."

"Claire? She told me she was sixteen! Yes I have seen her once or twice but there's nothing to it I assure you. If I'd known she was only fourteen I wouldn't have gone near her, I'm not that desperate."

"You're not the one who got her pregnant, are you? If I thought you were I'd make life hell for you, believe me."

"Not me, if she is pregnant it definitely wasn't me, I never got nearly that far. Your Claire's a tease and knows what it's all about, so's her friend, Kerry. They're both a handful and Claire probably got what she was asking for. For a fourteen year old she seems to have lots of experience."

Stan Hollingsworth couldn't believe what he was hearing. His baby, for she wasn't much more than that in his eyes, being described more or less as a nymphomaniac! It couldn't be. He couldn't understand how it could have happened. What could possibly make a lovely young girl like his daughter behave in the way this youngster was describing? He and Freda had bestowed all their love on her from the day she was born.

The wind was taken out of his sails completely. He was at a loss as to what to say to this boy. He couldn't tell Freda any of this, it would finish her. Claire was her life.

"What's your name?" he asked finally.

"Phil Jameson." came the reply, "Look I'm sorry I told you those things about Claire," he said as he saw the look of despair on Stan Hollingsworth's face, "but to be accused out of the blue of making your daughter pregnant made me see red. I've been through a lot lately and that was the last straw."

"Phil Jameson! You're the one the police are looking for! You were one of the robbers who killed Pete and here you are, as bold as brass, enjoying yourself in the park and telling me lies about my Claire. You were in it with Tim Priestley weren't you? He knew Claire too, I can't believe the scum she seems to have got involved with. For all I care you should have gone the same way as Priestley perhaps then we would all be better off. It was either you or him who got her pregnant. I'll have you up for rape as well as robbery."

"You've got it all wrong!" Jameson shouted as Hollingsworth made a grab for him, "It wasn't like that. You're messing it all up, leave me alone!"

"Hollingsworth's made his move, Guv," came the voice over the radio, "We're going in!"

"A car's on its way to you," said the Inspector, "bring them both in, we'll soon get things wrapped up now."

As the police bore down on the pair by the lake two of them grabbed hold of Hollingsworth and forced his arms behind his back handcuffing his wrists together. One of the policemen took his warrant card out of his pocket, held it in front of the startled man's face and said, "Stanley Hollingsworth, you are being arrested for assault. You do not have to say anything. It may harm your defence if you fail to mention something when questioned that you later rely on in court. Anything you say may be taken down and used in evidence."

Jameson called out "No, No, you've got the wrong one, He's not Jimmy! Everything has gone wrong." but his pleading was ignored and they were both bundled into the police car which had now arrived, and were taken to West Town police station.

While they were awaiting the arrival of the car Detective Sergeant Tully said to the Inspector, "Something doesn't feel right to me here, Guv, It's only a hunch but I hope we haven't made a mistake."

Stan Hollingsworth had regained his composure during the drive from the park and was objecting very strongly and very noisily to being taken to West Town police station. As he was led to the duty sergeant to be booked in and have his details taken he bellowed "What's this all about? Why have I been brought here? Nobody will tell me anything. What's going on?"

"All right, All right," said the duty sergeant, "if you'll quieten down for a minute perhaps we can get this sorted out. Will one of you go and get D.S. Tully, he knows all about this. Now sir, if you will please empty your pockets."

Having heard all the noise, Detective Inspector Harty and Detective Sergeant Tully were already on their way down to the charge room, anxious to get things moving and determine whether or not Hollingsworth was indeed Jimmy. As they entered the interview area Phil Jameson turned towards the Inspector.

"They've made a mistake Inspector!" he exclaimed, "They've messed it all up. This isn't Jimmy. I haven't seen him before."

"If that's the case," said the Inspector looking across at Hollingsworth, "why did he accost you in the park?

From what I heard he seems to know you and my men saw him grab you. Now why would he do that?"

"He accused me of making his daughter pregnant but it wasn't me. All right, I've seen his daughter, Claire, a few times and, apparently, he's seen me with her but I didn't make her pregnant. I've only ever walked with her and kissed her a couple of times. I had no idea she was pregnant."

"It must have been either him or that Tim Priestley, I'm sure of it." bellowed Stan Hollingsworth, "no girl's safe these days while blokes like them are roaming the streets, and she's only fourteen, why can't they look for girls their own age?"

"But Tim Priestley isn't roaming the streets any more, is he?" interjected Sergeant Tully.

"She told me she was sixteen, Inspector," said Jameson, "and she looked a lot older than fourteen which Mr Hollingsworth now says she is, but I never had sex with her anyway, never got the chance, so I certainly didn't get her pregnant. What are you going to do now about catching Jimmy? We don't know whether he saw what happened in the park, do we?"

"Hey," shouted Hollingsworth having heard this last remark, "you didn't think I had anything to do with the robbery, did you? I told you Pete Thompson was a good mate of mine. I wouldn't have done anything to harm him and, anyway, I would have been stupid to rob my own bus, wouldn't I?"

Ignoring Hollingsworth and replying to Jameson the Inspector said, "If you're right and this isn't Jimmy then we'll carry on with our original plan. We shall have to assume that he didn't witness the events in the park and, anyway, I can't see that too much harm has been done. It's still early afternoon. You get out there and do what we talked through earlier. No, wait, just in case anyone sees you leaving the station, Bob here will take you round the back and get you dropped off somewhere quiet in an unmarked car. You are supposed to have escaped from us earlier, nobody saw you coming in just now, we can't have you just walking out of here."

Turning to Sergeant Tully he said, "OK Bob? You heard that? When you get back we can spend our time with Mr Hollingsworth and get things sorted out with him. There could still be a very good reason for Jameson to deny that he is Jimmy."

To the duty sergeant he said, "Put Mr Hollingsworth in interview room two. I assume he has been told his rights and that he can have a solicitor present if he wants to?"

"Yes, Guv. He doesn't want a solicitor at the moment. He says he's got no reason to need one"

As Jameson walked to the rear car park with Sergeant Tully he thought to himself, "Well, at least I know for certain now the police are out there with me. If I do meet up with Jimmy this time I shall feel a bit more confident. I only hope it's still daylight if I do, it'll be easier for him to do something nasty to me in the dark."

The Sergeant took him to a quiet side road near the park and, before dropping him off, told him to stay where his followers could easily reach him and not to go for any more boat rides.

As the car moved off to return to the police station Jameson looked around but again could see no definite sign that he was being followed. He left the side road, turned right and crossed over the road so that he was walking along by the railings round the perimeter of the park. It was now nearly three thirty and children were leaving school and making their way through the park on the way home. There were schools on two sides of the park so that, compared to the quiet and tranquillity earlier in the day, it was now a bustle of activity with children of all ages, some accompanied by adults many of whom had taken their dogs along with them for their daily walk. He was sure that even Jimmy wouldn't dare to make a move with so many people about so felt that he could afford to relax a little. He realised that he had had nothing to eat since mid-morning, knew there was a snack bar in the park and made his way towards it.

He felt much better after a cheese and tomato sandwich and a polystyrene cup of luke warm tea so decided, at last, to follow the Inspector's instructions and make his way to the more secluded part of the park where Tim Priestley had been found. The South Gate entrance was for pedestrians only but came off a road which boasted large Edwardian houses on the side opposite the park. These were owned mainly by successful professional people with plenty of money. The road itself formed part of the number thirty-nine bus route and the buses passed down it every thirty minutes or so. That part of the park, which ran the full length of the road, was quite heavily wooded with oak, elm and beech trees and a stream from the lake threaded its way through the trees. The stream became no more than a shallow ditch as it approached the South Gate entrance and was largely hidden from sight by shrubs and bushes. It was here that Priestley had been found. Jameson, of course, didn't know the exact spot but that didn't matter anyway, he doubted that Jimmy would be around there, he'd hardly do another murder in the same place.

Very few people used the woods, usually couples out to take a dog for an evening walk or children who wanted to climb the trees. The South Gate entrance itself was used mainly by people wanting to get from one side of the park to the other, it was the easiest way to get to the railway station from the number thirty-nine bus route.

Phil Jameson walked aimlessly through the woods, following the stream, and throwing in the occasional pebble to watch the ripples spread. He looked for signs of wildlife, perhaps a squirrel or a rabbit, but could see nothing, even the birds appeared to give the area a miss. He remembered it had been the same when he had come here as a boy and wondered what it was they didn't like about it. He felt suddenly alone and looked around him for the policemen who should be following him but again could see nothing. They must be there somewhere but it made him wonder.

He came to a small rustic bridge over the stream and as he crossed it noticed a bench on the other side, he sat down, put his elbows on his knees, cupped his chin in his hands and, watching the clear water in the stream running over the pebbles, let his thoughts wander.

A hand on his shoulder broke his daydreaming but, before he could turn to see who it was, a stabbing pain suddenly shot through his shoulder and down his back. He gave a sharp cry then a dark mist formed over his eyes as he slumped to the ground and passed out.

Chapter twenty one

Harry Davies breathed a sigh of relief as he left Stan Hollingsworth at the fork in the paths in the park. Under normal circumstances he would have welcomed Stan's company, particularly on such a pleasant afternoon, but today he had a lot on his mind. He also had a headache and was feeling rather depressed, funerals invariably had that effect on him, not that he had attended all that many but he had been to enough.

It was because of the effect it had on him that he had left the burial site before the coffin had been lowered into the grave and returned to his bus to await the return of the others. He was therefore unaware of the small drama of the police message concerning the escape of Jameson from the funeral of Frank Prescott which had been overheard by all the other mourners.

He had no intention of returning home just yet, that had simply been an excuse to part company from Stan Hollingsworth. He was neither in the mood for tinkering with cars nor for Sylvie's idle chatter, as much as he loved being with her. He just wanted to be alone and do what he had to do.

As he had turned to give a cursory wave of goodbye to Stan he had spotted a boat on the lake with a solitary occupant. It was too far from where he was standing to recognise the person in the boat but something about the figure had seemed familiar to him.

He continued to walk along the path, which curved at an angle away from the lake, as he did not want to risk attracting Hollingsworth's attention. He lost sight of the lake as the path dipped down a grassy slope and through a copse but, after a further hundred yards or so, he found himself on a ridge with an almost panoramic view of the lake and the surrounding parkland. The distance was still too great for recognition of individual detail but he could see the unmistakeable figure of Stan Hollingsworth on the landing stage by the lake gesturing to the lone oarsman who was rowing towards him.

Davies stood and watched as the boat glided alongside the landing stage. He saw the attendant leave the small hut, go to the boat, pull it into the side with a long pole and bend down to make it secure while its occupant clambered out. He also saw Hollingsworth approach the person who had been in the boat and the two were now facing each other, obviously talking. Hollingsworth started to gesticulate rather wildly while the other continued to stand in front of him. Davies wondered what was going on and wished that he could hear what was being said. He was by now certain that he knew the person from the boat and was intrigued that Hollingsworth also knew him and apparently had something against him.

Suddenly Hollingsworth made a move which, from where Davies was standing, looked as though he was going to attack the man he had been speaking to. Then, to the amazement of Davies, three men he had not previously noticed ran quickly down to the landing stage from different directions. Two of them accosted Hollingsworth while the third approached the man he had been speaking to. Davies sat down on the grass to continue to watch from his vantage point. All that was happening was completely unexpected and was giving him plenty of food for thought.

After about five minutes had passed a police car arrived on the scene, Hollingsworth and the man from the boat were put into it and the three men who had apparently arrested them separated and walked away as the police car drove off. Davies remained sitting where he was to think about the events he had just witnessed.

Harry Davies did not know how long he had been sitting there after the police car had departed but he guessed that it must have been at least half an hour, probably longer. He had made up his mind what he was going to do and stood up to take stock of his bearings. He knew there was a pavilion not far from the lake where he could get a cup of tea and made his way towards it. After sitting in the afternoon sun for so long he needed refreshment before he could think of doing anything else.

While he sat at a table outside the pavilion with his cup of tea his mind returned again to the scene by the side of the lake. Although he had not been able to see at all clearly he had been certain that the man in the boat had been young Jameson, but now he was not so sure. How would Hollingsworth know him and why would Hollingsworth get so angry with him? It didn't make sense. Davies could only think that perhaps it was someone who had given Stan some trouble on the bus, there had been a lot of loutish behaviour towards bus crews just lately.

His thoughts then went to wonder why the police were so quickly on the scene. Who were they watching? Or were they just in the park looking out for trouble anyway? It seemed to him that that was very unlikely but surely they weren't watching Hollingsworth? The only reason they would be watching him was if they had good reason to think that he was the one who had held up the bus and killed Pete Thompson and the other two. Harry Davies knew that Hollingsworth hadn't done it, he couldn't, he hadn't got it in him to do anything remotely like that. If the police were watching the man in the boat then it was very unlikely that it could have been Jameson. After all, he reasoned, if the police knew where Jameson was he would be safely under lock and key, not enjoying himself on a sunny afternoon boating on the lake in the park.

Feeling thoroughly confused and unsettled Harry Davies drank the last of his tea, rose from his seat at the table and walked away from the pavilion. He decided to spend the remainder of the afternoon exploring the park. It was something he had wanted to do since first moving into the area but, somehow, had never found the time, he had always been too busy. At the same time he could be alone to think more deeply about the things he had seen this afternoon and try to fit the pieces together.

The park was large and spacious and in parts quite picturesque. The footpath past the boating lake linked the North and South gates and was used by the local population as a handy short cut from one part of town to the other, from the mainly residential area to the new shopping complex and vice versa. By now the schools were beginning to empty and this part of the park was becoming quite crowded with children and their parents. The boating lake and the recreation area next to it, both of which Harry knew well, formed the eastern boundary of the park anyway so he made his way westward to the seclusion of the ornamental lake and gardens.

He marvelled at the colourful profusion of flowers and shrubs as he wended his way slowly round the winding paths of the gardens and wondered why it was so difficult for the ordinary home gardener to achieve results like that. Not that he was a gardener himself, far from it, he left all that sort of thing to Sylvie. She was the one with the green fingers but, for all her hard work and as nice as it looked, it never ended up looking anything like this. Lack of money, he guessed, like everything else. Why did everything have to come down to money, or the lack of it, in the end?

The path he was on led, ultimately, to the ornamental lake which turned out to be quite a bit larger than he had expected. Silver birches, weeping willows and a host of other trees overhung its banks. It was dotted with small islands also bearing trees, mostly willows, the branches of which proved to be a haven for a surprising variety of birds. On the ultra calm water swam swans, ducks, geese and moorhens while the occasional dragonfly darted over its surface. The sun made a valiant effort to penetrate the foliage over the lake and sent rays reflecting off the water to give an almost unnatural brightness to some of the lower branches of the trees. The overall effect was one of complete serenity which made Harry feel almost as if he was trespassing where he did not belong.

He sat down on a rustic bench at the edge of the lake and, with his elbows resting on his knees and his hands clasped in front of him, surveyed the scene. Sitting there he felt that he could easily forget all his troubles and let the quietness and solitude overtake him.

"Why can't the whole of life be just like this?" he said to himself. "Why does everything have to be so complicated all the time?"

His mind wouldn't rest however and he found himself thinking of the things he had been forced to do over the past few days and the effect the bus robbery and subsequent killings had had on everybody he knew and wondered what the final outcome would be. It wouldn't be good whichever way you looked at it. He recognised that his own shortcomings had perhaps contributed in some way but didn't want to ponder on that. He couldn't see that anything he had done could have been done any differently, the end result would have been the same anyway.

He reluctantly rose from his seat and made his way round the edge of the lake until he reached a small rustic bridge which crossed a stream taking water from the lake to another part of the park. He crossed the bridge and found himself on a footpath which led to the wooded area near the South gate.

He entered the wood and picked up a fallen branch as he walked through the leaf strewn grounds. He seemed to have the place to himself, it was so quiet. He had expected to see schoolboys playing and climbing amongst the trees. Perhaps they didn't do that sort of thing any more, it was all videos and computer games these days. What a waste! Then he spotted someone sitting alone on a bench under the trees about fifty yards ahead. The man was sitting with his back towards Davies but he definitely recognised him this time. It was Phil Jameson without a doubt. So it must have been somebody else he had seen earlier on the boating lake. That man had been taken away in the police car, he would hardly likely be back in the park so soon.

Harry didn't want to frighten Jameson off, he had to get to him. Jameson was the only one left who had the answers. Harry was walking softly towards the bench when he spotted some movement among the trees.

The radio in Inspector Harty's office at West Town suddenly sparked into life.

"Christ, the bastard's got Jameson," came the voice, "where the hell did he come from? We need an ambulance quick, Guv, down by the South gate. The other two have got him."

"The ambulance is on its way," replied the Inspector watching Sergeant Tully who already had the telephone to his ear, "what do you mean the other two have got him? Make yourself clear. Have you got Jimmy? Is Jameson badly hurt? How the hell did it happen?"

"Sorry, Guv, it all came as a surprise. Yes, we've got the man who stabbed Jameson, we assume it's probably

Jimmy but there's no way of knowing. Jameson was stabbed in the back and is out cold. It looks as though he has lost a lot of blood but he's breathing ok, I think he's going to be all right, it doesn't look as though any vital organs can be damaged. We grabbed the man before he had a chance to strike again, he just suddenly appeared out of nowhere, we didn't stand a chance."

"OK," said the Inspector, "we'll have a full report when you get in. The ambulance should be with you soon. I'm sending a car, it will be at the park within minutes. One of you go to the hospital with Jameson, the other two bring the man in. Make absolutely sure there's no way he can get away, this business is bad enough as it is."

Turning to Detective Sergeant Tully the Inspector said, "What is this man, Bob, Superman or something? He gets to Jameson and stabs him right under the noses of three of our best men. It sounds as if he's slipped up this time though, didn't do too good a job on Jameson by all accounts, thank goodness. If Jimmy had killed him we'd have a hard job proving he had anything to do with the robbery or the other murders."

"It was a risk we had to take, Guv," replied Sergeant Tully, "and Jameson did a good job acting as bait, let's hope it has finally paid off. It will probably be a while before Jameson is fit enough to identify Jimmy for us as it is. The Chief's not going to be very happy, still, it could have been worse and I can't see what else we could have done."

"Let's wait until they bring him in before we say anything to the Chief, Bob. I don't know about you but I shall be very interested to see who it is."

Chapter twenty two

It was late evening before Phil Jameson came out of his coma and it took several minutes for him realise where he was. He was in a ward of West Town General Hospital, lying in a bed with the surrounding curtains closed and with a drip and various monitors attached to his body. For a moment he wondered what he was doing there then remembered sitting on the park bench and feeling the stabbing sensation in his back. So Jimmy had got to him after all but, apparently, unlike the others, he wasn't dead!

A nurse pulled the curtains apart and looked in. "Ah," she said, "so you're awake at last. You're a very lucky boy you know, the doctor will be along to see you in a minute. Are you in any pain?"

"I, I don't think so, " said Jameson, "although I do ache a little bit. It feels as though I've been thumped between the shoulder blades. Can I have a drink please, I'm very thirsty. My mouth feels like it's full of blotting paper."

"Sorry," said the nurse, "I'm afraid you'll have to wait until the doctor's seen you, he won't be long. There's someone waiting outside to see you too. She's been very worried about you."

"Who is it?" he asked, "Is it my mum?"

"It's Mrs Parkin, she says she's your Aunt Audrey, she's longing to come in and see you but we've got to wait for the doctor first."

"So," thought Jameson to himself, "Mum can't even be bothered to come to see me when I'm in hospital, not even when I've almost been killed." He suddenly felt terribly alone.

The doctor appeared after a few minutes and after checking him over said, "Another inch or so and you wouldn't be here, my lad. You have been very lucky but you must be kept very quiet for a couple of days."

"What happened Doctor?" Jameson asked, "I felt this pain in my shoulder but I didn't see anyone or anything. I must have passed out, I don't remember a thing after that."

"You were stabbed in the shoulder with a long sharp instrument," replied the doctor, "It penetrated deep but not far enough, fortunately, to do too much harm. If it had been a little lower down it would have been a different story. As it is you've lost a lot of blood and won't be able to use that arm properly for some time but, after a couple of days rest, and I mean that, you must rest, you should be as right as rain. You must count your blessings!"

"When I think of the others who weren't so lucky, especially my mate Frankie who had a horrible end, I know I've got a lot to be thankful for." said Jameson.

"His Aunt is waiting outside, Doctor," said the nurse, "is it all right for her to come in now?"

"I can't see any reason why not," said the doctor, "but no more than fifteen minutes and no other visitors before tomorrow afternoon."

Audrey Parkin entered the ward with a broad smile on her genial face and planted a kiss on Jameson's forehead.

"We've been so worried about you, Phil," she said, "you've been such a silly boy, but never mind, it's all over now. I wish you had come to me at the beginning, you know you're always welcome, I'm sure we could have worked something out."

"Have the police got Jimmy?" he asked.

"They've got the man who stabbed you, he's safely locked up now, but they need you to tell them whether he's the right one or not. The one who made you hold up that bus and who shot the bus driver. Don't worry about that now though, you concentrate on getting better. You can come and live with me and the girls when you come out of hospital. That is if you want to of course."

"Won't I have to go to prison?"

"Well, that's for a judge or magistrate to decide, but let's look on the bright side, the police are very pleased with you and that nice Inspector Harty is very sorry you got hurt. Between you and me I think everything will be all right, we'll just have to wait and see. A policeman's going to wait outside the ward until you're well enough to identify the man who stabbed you. That's just in case the man they've got isn't Jimmy not because they think you might run away again. You wouldn't be that silly."

"Isn't mum coming to see me?" asked Jameson, "I don't expect dad to but I thought mum might come."

"I expect she will come, Phil. You know what your dad's like, as obstinate as a bull and won't give an inch. He answers the 'phone every time I ring. I haven't been able to talk to your mum yet and he won't pass on any messages, all he keeps saying is 'I haven't got a son' and puts the 'phone down. I'll go round and try to see your mum when I leave here."

"Thanks, Aunt Audrey, I wish you were my mum, everything would be all right then."

The nurse came back at that moment and said, "Sorry Mrs Parkin, Phil must have some rest now, you can come back tomorrow afternoon if you want to."

"Goodbye, Phil," said Audrey Parkin, "you look after yourself and have a good sleep. I'll see what I can do. Perhaps I might be able to bring your mum along tomorrow, you never know."

Phil felt very tired but much happier having spoken to his Aunt Audrey and quickly settled into a deep sleep.

At West Town police station Detective Inspector Harty was talking to Detective Sergeant Tully. Both of them had spent the past few hours interviewing the man who had stabbed Jameson and taking statements from the policemen who had been trailing him in order to find out just how all three of them had managed to miss seeing Jimmy until it was almost too late.

"Well, Bob," said the Inspector, "there's very little doubt that we have the right man at last but we still need Jameson to formerly identify him for us. I rather fancy that he will be found to be insane and will probably end up in a mental institution. Like a lot of people in that state he's been extremely clever and devious, he's pulled the wool over a lot of people's eyes but, in the end, he was just that little bit too clever."

"Yes, Guv," replied the Sergeant, "it was ingenious the way he hoodwinked our three men. It looks as though he could have been trailing Jameson from the moment he entered the park but none of the three were aware he was there. Mind you they were distracted at the time of the stabbing and they can't really be blamed for that, there was very good reason."

"Nevertheless it looks as though we shall have to give our tracking methods a good overhaul, Bob. Like you I don't think we can attach any blame to our men under the circumstances but it does rather leave egg on our faces. It was pure luck, and the speed of our men at that moment that prevented a more serious ending. Do we know yet when Jameson will be fit enough to help us tie the loose ends?"

"I telephoned the hospital about half an hour ago, Guv. Jameson came out of his coma about twenty minutes before I 'phoned and has already had a short visit from his aunt. He's asleep at the moment. Apparently he's got

DEATH ON ROUTE 37

to have complete rest but should be ready for us the day after tomorrow."

"Right, we've got plenty to hold our man on until then. There's nothing more we can do here. Let's call it a day."

At that moment there was a call from the duty sergeant. "Oh good, you're still here, Inspector," he said, "I have a couple of young ladies here who are anxious to see you. Their names are Claire Hollingsworth and Kerry Matthews."

The following afternoon Jameson had the second visit from his Aunt Audrey. This time she was accompanied by another woman, his mother.

"My, you're looking much better than you did yesterday, Phil," said Audrey Parkin, "and just look who I've brought with me, the best medicine you can have I reckon."

Mrs Jameson approached her son with tears in her eyes and bent down to kiss him. "I'm so sorry, Phil," she said, "I've been so worried about you. I didn't want any of it to happen. I didn't want you to leave home but I've been so weak. I've allowed your father to ride roughshod over everyone but it won't happen again, I promise. I'm so pleased to see you, I've really missed you. I nearly fainted when Audrey told me what had happened."

"I don't really blame you, mum." he replied, "Dad's never liked me, he's always made that clear, but I couldn't understand why you wouldn't stand up for me. I think I understand now. What are you going to do?"

"I've left him Phil. I should have done it years ago but I suppose I've been too frightened to. Aunt Audrey's offered to put me up for the time being. I'm divorcing your dad."

Phil Jameson put his good arm round his mother and held her close, there were tears in his eyes now.

Everything was working out far better than he could ever have expected.

"Good for you mum." he said.

At ten o'clock on Friday morning the doctor proclaimed that Phil Jameson was fit enough to go to West Town police station to identify the man they were holding. Detective Inspector Harty and Detective Sergeant Tully collected him from the hospital personally and drove him to the police station in their car.

As they entered the room where Jameson was to confront the man the Inspector said, "We know that we have the right man, I will tell you how when you have confirmed his identity. We need, however, your confirmation because without it, apart from the stabbing of you which was witnessed first-hand by three of our most reliable men, the evidence against him for the robbery on the bus and the murders of Thompson, Prescott and Priestley is largely circumstantial. Are you sure you are well enough to go through with it?"

"Yes, Inspector," Jameson said, "absolutely sure. I owe it to Frankie to have him locked away. I can't let Frankie down a second time."

"Right, Bob," said the Inspector, "bring in the suspect."

To Jameson he said, "Now be absolutely sure that this is the man who involved you and the others in the robbery on the bus. You won't be doing anyone any favours if you identify the wrong man."

As the Sergeant led in a surly looking man with hands cuffed behind his back, Jameson gave an involuntary gasp and without any hesitation said, "Yes, that's him, that's Jimmy, that's the man who killed Frankie and burnt him in the car."

The Inspector nodded to Sergeant Tully who took the man out of the room and led him back down to the cells.

"It was the name, Jimmy, that misled us all along." the Inspector said to Jameson, "For a long time, in fact right up to the moment you were stabbed, we were sure that Harry Davies was the man we were after. I believe you know him, He has told us now that you have spent some time in the past working with him on his cars. He hasn't been completely honest with us, you see. Everything we had seemed to point in his direction, opportunity, the means, the motive. There was no evidence, however, to confirm our suspicions. Then, by a remarkable coincidence, Harry Davies was seen in the park by the three policemen following you. He was approaching you in a very suspicious manner as you sat, completely unaware, on the bench in the woods. This seemed to our three men to confirm absolutely our suspicions and their eyes were on him totally as he drew closer to you waiting for his final move. Then, to everybody's surprise, Jimmy jumped out from the trees and stabbed you. Apparently he had been so intent on watching you in case you moved that he hadn't seen Davies approaching. He certainly hadn't seen our men but they are trained to become almost invisible in their surroundings. Fortunately they were close enough to you to grab Jimmy before he could strike a second time."

"The use of the name, Jimmy, fooled everyone, including myself, it was a real red herring, didn't seem to fit any of our suspects. It just did not occur to any of us that it was not Jimmy at all but the initials G.M. with the 'y' added as an embellishment. Geoff Matthews in fact, the family man, a man who had no apparent motive for robbery, nor for murder, especially of his own cousin, Pete Thompson."

"Then why did he do it?" asked Jameson, "and why involve me and the others? Why on earth did he murder Frankie Prescott?"

"We wondered about that too," said the Inspector, "until, the day before yesterday. I had a visit from his daughter, Kerry, and her friend, Claire Hollingsworth. I believe you know them both. What they told me, coupled with other evidence gathered over the past couple of weeks, finished the jigsaw and put all the pieces in the right place."

"Pete Thompson," continued the Inspector, "was not a very nice man although this was not known at all by Stan Hollingsworth and only suspected by Geoff Matthews. Claire and Kerry had been taken out regularly, with their parents' consent, by Pete Thompson over a number of years. What nobody knew, or suspected, was that Thompson was a member, in fact the leader, of a paedophile ring and had been abusing the girls and involving them in various sexual activities from a very early age."

"That's disgusting!" exclaimed Jameson, "why on earth didn't they say anything or tell their parents?"

"That's very easily said," replied the Inspector, "But these people have a very thorough hold over their victims who don't like what's happening to them but live in fear of being found out. They are made to feel so guilty they come to believe they are responsible for what is happening. The death of Thompson and the arrest of her father made Kerry Matthews realise the truth and she persuaded Claire Hollingsworth to come with her to see me. It was Thompson, you see, who made Claire pregnant, not Priestley nor yourself, as you very well know."

"Does Claire's father know that?"

"He does now and he's a very unhappy man. He can't understand how he was fooled by Thompson for all those years. He did not remotely suspect that Thompson was involved in anything like that nor that his daughter could allow herself to be used in that way but, of course, she was very young when it started and could do nothing to stop Thompson. Although we were sure in our own minds, wrongly as we now know, that Davies was our man we also suspected that Hollingsworth might be Jimmy and, at one point, things looked quite black against him but, as we have discovered since, he was totally oblivious to anything that was going on and was simply a man engrossed in his own life. He was genuinely sorry that Thompson was dead but some of his subsequent actions, although quite innocent, made us suspicious."

"If Geoff Matthews didn't know about Thompson either what made him do it?" asked Jameson.

"Well, Hollingsworth is a family man too who loves his wife and daughter and has all the normal parental fears which come with a healthy, growing, inquisitive teenage girl. That's why he accosted you in the park. He had no idea of the horrors his daughter had already endured for much of her young life and it never occurred to him that his friend, Thompson, could be anything other than he appeared to be. Matthews, on the other hand, was obsessed with the idea that his daughter, Kerry, should remain 'pure and innocent'. At fourteen she is blossoming into a very attractive young lady and the very thought of anybody touching her drove him crazy. Thompson was in the habit of taking her out whenever he could, ostensibly to a cinema or to the shops, sometimes alone and sometimes with her friend, Claire. Matthews had no real reason to suspect anything out of the ordinary, he certainly had no knowledge of Thompson's perversions, but had a feeling that the relationship between his daughter and Thompson was not what it should be. Jealousy probably caused that feeling to fester in his mind until he convinced himself that he must get rid of Thompson. It was then that he thought up the idea of the bus robbery. He actually had no real interest in robbing the bus passengers, it was simply a means to an end, to kill Thompson. That was another thing that misled us. We were working on the assumption from the beginning, falling right into the trap that Matthews had set for us, that the robbery was the intended crime and that the killing of the driver was the unfortunate outcome of the use of guns by inexperienced men. Mr Watkins being on the bus with the week's takings from the newsagents, which you relieved him of, reinforced that assumption and made it difficult to consider an alternative motive.

In fact, as we now know, the murder of Thompson was the main intention all along, the robbery was just a blind, probably a game to Matthews which is how he explained it to you. His major problem was the timing of the robbery but that was handed to him on a plate the very weekend he had already been through the plans with you, Prescott and Priestley. On the Sunday morning of that weekend Thompson called round to his house to cancel a trip which had already been arranged with Kerry Matthews on the following Tuesday. Hollingsworth wanted to finish a DIY project he had been working on and had asked Thompson to take over his shift on that day on the number thirty-seven bus. Matthews had used the number thirty-seven route into town on a number of occasions and knew it well. He knew of Birstal Drive, the quiet road where the robbery was carried out, and that it was ideal for his purposes. He also knew that his newsagent, Mr Watkins, usually visited the bank on Tuesdays and used the number thirty-seven bus to do so. He made a point of having a chat with the newsagent every day when he picked up his morning paper and it was a simple matter to confirm that the same would happen on that Tuesday without raising Mr Watkins' suspicions. People unwittingly give out all sorts of information without considering the consequences when they get together for an idle chat, you know. That fact was well recognised during the war and often used to advantage."

"But why did he involve us?" asked Jameson. "I've been asking myself that question a lot."

"It was no accident that he chose you and Priestley to take part in the robbery. That has become quite clear now that we know the full story. As you know Hollingsworth had seen you with his daughter, Claire, and had jumped to the wrong conclusions. He had it out with you by the boating lake the other afternoon. Matthews had also seen his daughter, Kerry, with you and Tim Priestley, on separate occasions because, at that time, you and Priestley were unknown to each other. To him, you were both as much of a threat to his daughter as Thompson was. By staging the robbery on a double decker bus you were a major element in a major crime involving the use of firearms. If things went wrong and he couldn't kill you both as well as Thompson, which was always his intention by the way, at least you would both be arrested and would probably be locked away for a long time. That would have the desired effect of keeping you away from his precious Kerry.

To stage the robbery properly, however, he needed a fourth member and this is where you brought your friend, Frank Prescott, into the picture. It was indeed unfortunate for him that he had recently lost his job, otherwise, I'm sure, he would never have become involved. As it happens it was a bonus for Matthews. He now had an expert driver for the getaway and it didn't matter to him that Prescott was unknown to him. Any man was a potential threat to his daughter and should be put out of the way."

"Surely he didn't intend to kill every man, or boy, who had, or could have, any contact with Kerry?" asked Jameson. "He really must be sick in the head."

"Who knows what goes on in a mind like that?" replied the Inspector, "He's probably capable of anything. He had been bottling it all up for quite some time. We shall have to wait and see but I'm fairly certain that he will finish his days locked away in an institution."

"What will happen to Claire and Kerry?"

"Claire Hollingsworth is fortunate in that she has a caring father, as well as a mother to help her through the difficult time ahead but both girls will need counselling over the next few months. They have experienced things during the last few years that no child should endure. They now have to be taught what is right and what is wrong. The people who abuse children don't realise and don't care about the mental damage that is done. Their lives, unfortunately, have been irreparably scarred and it is really up to the pair of them to make the most of their future. If you see them again, and I'm not saying you shouldn't, bear that in mind and make allowances for their behaviour."

"When Kerry heard that her father had been arrested for the murder of Pete Thompson, and that we knew about Thompson's background, she persuaded Claire to come with her to tell me everything. That took enormous courage and is a credit to both of them. Claire confessed that Thompson had made her pregnant and they both gave details of abuse, mostly sexual, not only by Thompson but also by others they had been introduced to by him, since the age of five. With the information we gained from Thompson's computer system, and with the aid of the two girls, a lot of people have a lot to worry about."

"Can I ask, after all that," said Jameson, "what's going to happen to me?"

"Well," replied Detective Inspector Harty "that's ultimately for the courts to decide. You have, after all, committed a major crime and you will have to go to trial. Your part in it, however, was rather insignificant when compared to Matthews and will be overshadowed by his subsequent murders. If you can persuade the jury, as you have persuaded me, that all along you were under the impression you were involved in a rag day stunt or game of some sort you shouldn't have too much to worry about. There's just one more thing, though, that will go a long way towards deciding your fate."

"What's that, Inspector?"

"The proceeds from the robbery. We have most of the jewellery and credit cards that were taken, and some of the cash, but the bulk of the cash is still missing. You've already admitted to having it in your possession so what about it?"

"I was hoping you had forgotten that!" said Jameson smiling, "I'll see what I can do.".

THE END

2068965R00118

Printed in Great Britain
by Amazon.co.uk, Ltd.,
Marston Gate.